Beaver Creek Blues

tangled dreams and Telemark keys

Sherie Kleven-Jensen

Bloomington, IN  Milton Keynes, UK

authorHOUSE

AuthorHouse™
1663 Liberty Drive, Suite 200
Bloomington, IN 47403
www.authorhouse.com
Phone: 1-800-839-8640

AuthorHouse™ UK Ltd.
500 Avebury Boulevard
Central Milton Keynes, MK9 2BE
www.authorhouse.co.uk
Phone: 08001974150

This book is a work of non-fiction. Most of the circumstances within
this book occurred many years ago. The depiction of people, places
and situations is true, as experienced by the author at that time.

First published by AuthorHouse 12/7/2006

ISBN: 1-4259-1584-1 (sc)

Printed in the United States of America
Bloomington, Indiana

This book is printed on acid-free paper.

This book is dedicated to

Innocence and Imagination

and all other Endangered Species.

"We shall not cease from exploration
and the end of all our exploring
will be to arrive where we started
and know the place for the first time."

- T. S. Eliot

Beaver Creek Blues

Table of Contents

Section Three: WILD OATS TRAIL
(UND TO SACRAMENTO)

Section Four: HIDING IN THE WOODS
(HEALED, CONCEALED, REVEALED)

Section Five: TICKLING MY ROOTS

♎︎

A LITTLE INTRO

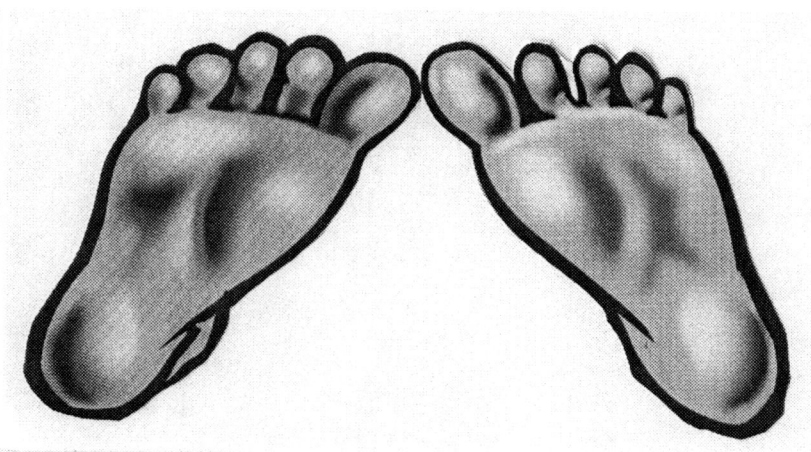

Happy Toes

*Nothing feels better than
Chow fur soft on my skin, or
the fledgling February sun and
brand new red underwear.
But these treasures do not fit
in the pocket of my work duds.
When I go to work, I am a poor
person with empty pockets
and plain-Jane underwear,
chewing on foofaraw until they
let me spit and kick my bare feet
back home,
where daydreams
are sculpted in canine design
and toes are the tools
for scribbling rhymes.*

April 2004

SIMBA ☺

Paisley Winds

See! The paw is
quicker than the eye.
Simba pops the lock of my
inflated poverty and
we plunge
from knuckle-scrubbed darkness
into a swirl of paisley winds,
mud bubbles and sun tails.
A crescendo of fir coats
adorns the belly of the sky;
the beat of bullfrogs
in the caramel pond
rises
and falls into a soft ruffle
at the nest of the King Tree;
his wooden gills stretch under my hug
and our breath becomes one.
I wonder, can my whispers travel
to the top of the King, where
my mother's eagle likes to rest?
Can I send her a message?

SIMBA & RUBY POSE AT CLIFF-TOP
WITH OUR "GNARLY WOOD"

For a moment, I am a candle, melting into
the tree, and my sunflower comrade
is a purring puddle at my feet.
A sudden Chinook snuffs out our sighs
and flattens the sky.
Simba zips up her purrs and heads south.
The moon has embroidered our trail, and
the red planet
was kind enough to leave the porch light on for us.

March 2004

*"To the south is Mars, and
to the east, the moon…
if Simba pulls me fast enough,
we'll reach one of them by noon."*

God Loves You
and so do I.
Hope you have a
wonderful day.
Love
Mom

Mom Dreams
(in the months after her passing)

March 18, 2003:

Can't they see she's smiling inside? She is absolutely tickled as they roll her down the sidewalk from the church. Her face shines in a new light that seems to come from deep behind her closed eyes. She looks like she wants to share her happiness but they aren't even looking at her; they are oblivious to the moment, the wonderful thing that is happening to her. How can they not see, not feel this? She is overflowing with exuberance and wants – *needs* to share...but they just keep rolling her and steer her into a big gray building, out of the sun.

Meanwhile, I keep trying to catch up but everything gets in my way. I don't get to the church on time, and the front door is blocked and when I finally get in through the back door, I can't find a place to sit and there are no programs left for me to see where they are at in the service and no one helps me. Then they roll her out and I can't catch up to her.

A bus picks me up, then stops and the driver points to a ladder that is supposed to get me to her if I hurry, but as I reach out to start climbing the ladder, it disappears, and I look down the street where I last saw her and realize no matter how fast I run, I'll never catch her.

April 6, 2003:

I am in the kitchen of Mom's little apartment in Sharon. There is a blue light shining through a glass window in the freezer door. Mom tells me to open the door and bring her the wooden box that's inside the light. She opens the box and pulls out two old necklaces: one looks like a chain of hemp loops, the other is a tarnished chain holding a large, broken gold letter. This one is very important to her; she puts it in my hand and insists that I take it. She wants me to fix it. I ask her what the broken letter is and she tells me to guess. I think it looks like a "D" and I ask her,

SHARON CENTENNIAL

JULY 5, 6, 7

1896 – 1996

SHARON NORTH DAKOTA

"Is it a "D" Mom?" but she will not answer me, she only puts it back into my hands and tells me that I must take it and fix it.

(I can only think of one "broken D" in Mom's life that worried her, it was her granddaughter Deanne who separated herself from the family.)

June 14, 2003:
I'm back in Sharon, ND, walking around town with business associates (I don't know them). I want to get away from them because all they talk about is taxes, but they follow me everywhere. Finally, I manage to lose them and I walk to the edge of town by myself, to the southwest corner where the slaughterhouse used to be, next to a slough. In place of the old slaughterhouse is a beautiful house, blue with gray trim, 2-story, humble by many standards, but to me in this dream, this house shines like the gates of heaven. The old muddy slough is now a brilliant, crystal blue lake which makes this house look even more like heaven.

I feel like I have found the answer to all my problems, right here. My search is over: I want this house! Even in my dream, my practical mind is asking *what* I would do for a living in the tiny town of Sharon, but I don't care, *I just want this house!*

I run back to the building where I know all the business associates are; one of them stops to chastise me because I am not participating. I push her aside, saying, "All you guys talk about is taxes, taxes, taxes, and I am sick of taxes!"

Then, I find my Mom, sitting along the back wall of the room. I tell her about the house; I want her to come and see it. I take her hands to help her up; it is important that she sees this house! She shakes her head; she can't come with me. I plead, I beg, but she says no, she can't. She looks down at her feet and I sense that it's not that she doesn't want to come with me, but she physically cannot leave that spot because there's something wrong with her feet?

(Maybe this was a warning dream to me. One year after Mom passed away, I "lost my feet". My hiking days were terminated by sudden, screaming pain in my ankles and my life became littered with confused doctors.)

Foot Amputation Dream (August, 2003):

I wake up in the gray light of a very busy corridor. I am disoriented; I don't know who the people are rushing about me, and I don't know why I'm there. I am on a stretcher. I don't feel any pain. I raise my head to look down over the white sheets covering my body. My feet are missing.

I am shocked; I am insulted that my feet would be removed without my permission. I want an answer, now! I don't see any buttons to push for help. I call out to the people walking around me, and they don't hear me; they don't even look at me. I stare at the bandaged stumps where my feet used to be and begin to panic. I call out more loudly; I demand an explanation of what has happened to my feet!

One doctor finally stops long enough to shake his head. He has a plastic bag in one hand and in his other hand there's a yellow bird in a cage. He tries to give me the bird cage but I don't want it. I want his plastic bag, because I know my feet are in there. He will not give it to me! He sets the bird cage on my lap, turns and walks away. I try to yell at him, but my voice only comes out in a whisper. The bird is beautiful and I know it is very intelligent. The cage disappears and the bird stays with me, walking up and down my legs, hopping from one side of my body to the other. I feel calm; I trust this bird. I try to listen because I think it can tell me something; I think it's important, but I can't hear over the loud hum of a motor coming in closer and closer from somewhere down the hall.

The loud motor is my ringing alarm clock.

♎

CHILD OF THE PRAIRIE

UNCLE MELVIN (RT)
IN HIS FREE-WHEELING DAYS

Prairie Reunion
(1977)

Neat grids of gravel roads greet the tires of her Ford; she relaxes in the familiar world of brown pastures and snow dusted fields. Her foot barely touches the accelerator as the clean, serene air fills her car, re-baptizing her in rich kindred intuition. These are the roads of her father, her first-grade teacher, her uncles. This was her great-grandma's prairie of choice. Time has not changed this landscape but for the petite telephone poles and the abandoned farms on every square mile.

Up ahead, to the left, weeds try to conceal two tire-tracks leading to a circle of buildings, gray and tired of being alone. She pulls in and steps out, fascinated by the stories hiding inside the emptiness. She imagines being greeted by the family dog, a housewife wrapped in an apron and a scattering of brown and white chickens. She gazes over the broken windows, the wooden steps to the front door, the rusty doorknob, and she can visualize how it once looked in the early morning light: flowers hugging the walk, lazy cats lounging near the door. The man of the house would be first to step outside each morning, wearing bibs, flannel and a warm scent of coffee, eggs and toast. His boots would cut a trail through new whiskers of dew on his way to the barn for morning chores. His cows would know the footsteps of their master before he opened the door to their curious faces. Meanwhile, inside the house, children would be waiting with jackets and backpacks for their 9-mile ride on a big yellow school bus to the nearest town. Where are these children today, and do they miss the walls of this sad old house?

Beaver Creek fills a corner of our pasture

Thousands of crystal snowflakes float into her reflections as the old cottonwoods awaken to a new breeze. A hawk, perched on the light-pole, becomes bored and flies away toward the creek. She follows the fence line until she sees the water. The sound, as it circles round rocks, is reassuring, an intimate whisper. She listens and knows that this is the voice that called her great-grandma and encouraged the prairie settlers; it is the reliable song of nature, cycling through the seasons. This is the ageless truth: every bird, tree, person and snowflake contributes to the tune of survival; we are a melody of generations moving in unbroken rhythm.

UNCLE TORGER WITH BABY NIECE THELMA

Tumbling Twig

I'm just a twig
off the old family tree.
My great uncle Torger
was exactly like me.
He loved pansy faces
and smooth pocket rocks;
he created new kingdoms
on each of his walks.

I am his twin
born 90 years late;
I'm the words to that tune
that he couldn't quite place.
I'm the rock in his tire
with a contagious new beat;
I'm the speck in his eye
that played hide-and-seek.

I'm the scent in his garden
before winter was gone,
and the firefly dust on the
jar by his yawn.
I was maybe a wink
at the end of his joke and
my eyes have a twist
of his teal shade of smoke.

The kids of Steele County
made his life complete;
they followed him home
like an itch on his feet.
He guided them over
a dreamless cocoon,
tossing pennies with wings,
introducing the moon.

His aura resides
in the waves of blue flax;
he's the last ripple
that will not relax, and
I'm always late 'cause
the rope on my knee
is knotted securely
to his century.

His legacy grows
more persistent than big
in the humming of pansies
and tumbling twigs.

5/06/03

Moon Landing
July 20, 1969

He's thinking: "Good thing this old '66 Ford Custom is built like a tank. It can take this beating."

She's thinking: "There's got to be something wrong with the steering on this beast! It doesn't want to stay on the road at all!"

He tells her to stop and let everyone (car, man, girl) rest for a bit. She adjusts the big livingroom pillow to boost herself up where she can almost see over the top of the steering wheel.

He asks her to try it again. Her foot eases up on the clutch pedal, the engine roars, belches, hiccups, and stops. Oops. She tries it again, a little more smoothly. They weave down the gravel road like a drunken snake. They are one mile east of the farm when he asks her to turn right. She's got it, she's mastered this man-beast, she turns, she knows the right wheel is gracefully hugging the corner...what!? Hey, whoa... doggone it; she has gracefully parked them in a nose-dive down in the ditch.

The car is idling in drive because she is standing on the clutch and brake pedals. He tells her to put it in reverse and back it out of there. He's not going to bail her out of this one. Her hands are sweaty. She puts the car in neutral to free her feet, pushing herself high up on her pillow, as if that will help raise the car. Her feet can't touch the pedals when she's up that high, so she slides back down where she can't

Uncle Helmer's reliable transportation

see the road behind her. She goes for it, determined not to let him down. The engine growls as she revs it and holds the clutch a little too long, but they move, backwards, up, up… aahh, there's the horizon again! She brakes, leaving them breathless, kitty-wompus in the middle of the road.

She looks at him. Is that a little smile? He says this is a good time to go back home and watch those space men on the moon.

The return mile is a little less delirious than the original mile. On the way, he says maybe he'll put her in the old truck out in the field and let her get used to the steering out there (where there are only haystacks to hit). That's how the "older girls" learned, he says.

The big ride ends just in time to go in to the house and see "One small step…" by Neil Armstrong.

This is the day when she discovered her own lunar landscape, in the corner ditch just outside the Windloss farm.

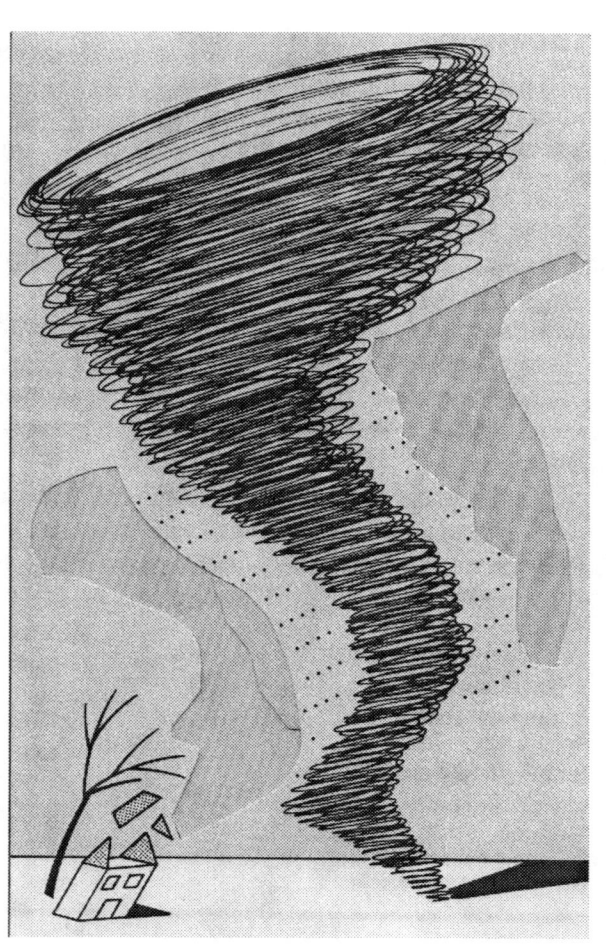

Twister

Elfonzo the red
elephant
falls
when his ride
on my
roller-coaster breathing
is intersected by
the erratic rattling
of my double-pane
windows.
Irritable
whirlwind ladders
slam the house and up
and down
and up against the well-sealed
ceiling
of a strong gray sky.
The stubborn swirl lands
on its feet and stomps
across the roof in a
stratospheric tantrum.

I hide under my
Hollie Hobbie bedspread
and pray for this monster
to find its break
between this suffocation
and that escape.

1975

A.R.Scherling
113 BROADWAY
FARGO, N.D.

UNCLE MONS & AUNT CLARA

Uncle Mons

"Every good Norwegian should have one of these; it's a good tool. I'm lucky I found this one," he smiled as he set his latest gadget on the table, just out of my reach.

It was another Sunday at the Stordahl's, with Mom and Aunt Clara in the kitchen, swapping ladies news of the week, and Dad, Uncle Mons and me at the big oak diningroom table. I stretched out of my chair and snatched the mystery tool for closer inspection. Mons leaned back, crossed his arms and watched me sleuth it out. There was a wooden base, holding a short stick and a long stick upright. There was a little chain with a tiny padlock connecting the two sticks. The sticks didn't move, the padlock didn't seem to be very important to the function of this thing, whatever it was. I shrugged and handed it to Dad who took the lock off, put it back on, turned it upside-down, and gave up.

"C'mon, don't you know a *pole-lock* when you see one?" Mons laughed as he went on to tell the adventure which led to this little discovery.

Mons should have been a roving reporter instead of a farmer. He loves going for drives to nowhere special, stopping in small cafés along the way, making friends everywhere, easily. He is

a great story teller, able to wrap new suspense and fun around a tale that's been told many times before. He specializes in ghost stories or crazy neighbor stories.

Mons has never lost the little kid who lives inside him, which makes him irresistible from a real kid's point of view. He can get a laugh and even some playfulness from stressed-out adults. His stories and his toys (polaroid cameras, tape recorders, pet rocks, wooden puzzles) can break any ice.

In summers when his grandson Burkley stays there, Mons builds a tower of tractor-tire inner tubes for us to bounce around on. He gets a kick out of diving down on the big tube and bouncing the rest of us over to a pile of smaller tubes. Then, he fires-up the tractor and gives us sky-rides on the hay scoop. He takes his gun collection out and carefully lets us shoot target practice in his open field. My favorite is the four-barrel pistol.

Every time he gets a new car, he hands me the keys and lets me drive it around the countryside! Mom and Dad are always in the back seat, and Mons is up front with me. They chat with each other while I enjoy the feel of a new car. I don't know why he trusts me so much, but I'm not complaining!

When I was little, Mons let me play with his violins. He would sing a silly song and dance around in circles while I squawked on the poor strings. He taught me how to "Do The Twist" and he taught me how to poker-face and strategize in Chinese Checkers and card games.

No one ever sits between Uncle Mons and Sherie; it is an unwritten rule, in their house or ours. We are buds. We are

Mons & Dad on a typical Sunday afternoon

always challenging each other's wit; we stand back-to-back and debate over who is the tallest, and I kid him about shrinking.

We always go to the Fargo Fair together, every August. Mons never goes on rides, but Dad does. Mons just likes the party atmosphere, I think. Dad says it's hard to get him to go home because he loves socializing over a drink or two. Or three. Or four. When Aunt Clara goes out alone with him, she ends up spending half the night sleeping in the car, waiting for him.

Nobody's perfect. Everybody has a bad habit or two but those habits aren't how we should define each person. We should describe someone's life based on their impact on other people. Mons stands out; he makes a difference, because he is spunky and he shows us how to find joy in little things that we wouldn't take time to see on our own.

What's life all about? Is it about getting all the chores done, or playing like a little kid again?

1973

BEAVER CREEK CHURCH

Pink Curlers

A colorful ensemble is ready to breathe life into her imagination. Sunday School book, teacher's manual, markers, construction paper and an experienced red Bible take position on the dining room table. The pupil's book is opened to a cartoon story with large, third-grader print. She concentrates on it as if she were a third-grader herself. Decorated in neat rows of pink plastic curlers, the top of her head gives only a glimpse of pendulum eyes behind the black-rimmed wings of her reading glasses.

This is my mom; this is Saturday night. She's been a Sunday School teacher for 23 years. We can predict her performance with 100% accuracy. Bowing to the clean supper dishes, she exits right, cuts a straight path through the livingroom, pivots left past the old brown davenport, lifts her book bag from the bedroom doorknob and turns, transformed. She is no longer a housewife. Now, she is a producer, and the dining room table is the stage where her Bible story comes to life.

Just five feet in front of her, the Saturday night TV shows slide by without distracting her. Now and then, she looks up at *The Lawrence Welk Show*, but she doesn't really see it.

Thelma
For flid og god opfösel,

CARD TO THELMA WHEN SHE WAS
A YOUNG STUDENT IN A
NORWEGIAN-SPEAKING CHURCH

Her thumbnail clicks softly against the pages of her teacher's manual. She finds the right one, writes a note in the margin and pushes the book to the side, exchanging it for purple and yellow construction paper. Tracing images with the concentration of a little girl, she carefully creates paper models of an ark and animals for her kids to imitate and decorate in their own way. She yawns, wiggles her fingers and leans heavily against the chair, lifting her feet up, stretching and twisting her ankles 'round and 'round. Her eyes never look up while she stretches. Satisfied, she drops her feet back to the floor and packs tomorrow's production into her bag.

On Sunday, we return from our morning at church and she serves up a noon meal of sandwiches and anecdotes from her inquisitive kids. She is proud; inspired by their honesty and intuition. The over-worked worries of the week go flying out the window and the light in her eyes invites us all, for a moment, to feel the fun, to be one with the young.

1975

BALLAD OF THE OUTHOUSE

There she was, a girl of eight,
at 4:00 a.m., wide awake;
cricket trails below the dew
kissed the ears on bunny shoes
running through the fading night
to the door without a light.
Once inside, with no delay,
hovering, she found her way
and almost sang a thankful sigh
until the monster caught her eye.
What! Don't breathe, don't even pee!
That's mama bear and family!
Her heartbeat calls them, like a drum...
what will happen when they come?
Frantically, she shuts the door;
she cannot hush the spooky roar
inside her head; it fills the room!
BOOM-BOOM! BOOM-BOOM-BOOM!
Oh no! They've come to take her soul!
She almost falls into the hole
but then a voice stops her un-gluing:

"Good Grief, girl, what ARE you doing?"
"Mom? Look out! You better hide!"
With that, Mom pushed the door inside
and grabbed a hand, so cold and white,
outside, to meet the golden light.
Pointing where the bears had been,
she didn't see Mom's little grin:
The Wagon, with its twisted tires,
upside-down, then inspired
shadows, clever with their time
to perpetrate this "grizzly" crime.

June 8, 2005
(A fun memory of my young imagination running away
in the early morning shadows.)

EARTH'S MOON

Moon

Floating mirror
with
sunken eyes, so
stern but soft
as
shine-white
clouds
drape past...
but fast,
like a
stick-pin
from its hole,
your leaving
closes
your entry.

September 1977

Walking with Calico

Memory, the gray magnet, tugs at the laces of his brown work boots. The westbound wind steers him down the gravel driveway from the house toward his barn. The road curves gently to the left as he passes the chicken coop. A guinea hen, perched on the roof of the well-house, scolds him for trespassing. The feeling is mutual. He bought a handful of guineas after all his leghorns were killed one night by a badger. These ugly birds aren't good for egg laying or anything else, but predators are said to be driven away by their shrill, raucous hullabaloo.

Ignoring the squawking has become easier. He may not pay attention if there ever is a real chicken emergency. He works his way to the south side of the barn and stops, reassured by the familiar panorama of pasture, resting crops and calm weather. Returning from another mysterious adventure, Calico, his best mouser, joins him and entwines herself around his feet. Looking up, he marvels at the one cupola standing strong, after losing its twin years ago. He sees even more green shingles missing from the roof. He tries not to let it bother him. No cows live in his barn anymore. The only residents are pigeons, mice, and barn cats. If he were younger, he knows that he could fix this barn up to be good as new. He walks under the two heavy beams holding up the wall. They are as strong as they were 25 years ago, planted deeply at a 45° angle, wedged against the leaning structure. He will never forget the twister that almost took his barn. It beared down on the farm like a mad bull, trampling everything in its path. It sucked his breath from his chest. Now, the family laughs over the memory of seeing him running across the farmyard and ducking just as the roof of the grain bin flew over his head like a flying saucer.

Dad's International Harvester tractor

He works his way back to the front of the barn, pausing at the criss-cross boards on the door to brush the blistered white paint with his strong, calloused hand. He can't stop the traces of time. Unhooking the latch, the door creaks open and Calico jumps over the doorstep ahead of him. The darkness inside fogs his eyes but he is familiar with the space around him. All silent. The raw cement floor spreads its chill upward through the coarse wooden beams. He tests them all and finds none as sturdy as it once was. The stall gates hold remnants of fur from generations of hungry calves who knew him as their surrogate mama. He remembers their names and personalities as if they were his children.

The old cream separator is sealed in cobwebs, but it is stainless-steel, and he knows it could be cleaned up to do the job for another season of milk cows. Next to the separator is the feed bin. The door swings up to show dusty corners of old corn meal, now the feast of gluttonous rats and mice. He smooths his hand over the wall next to the feed bin, tracing the durable carvings of old Uncle Pete. Pete was such a fidgety guy, and yet he had the patience to perfect this three-dimensional portrait of the barn with little stick chickens, pigs and horses, signed proudly by P.O. Touching this wall never fails to flood his mind with the characters who worked this farm through the years: hired-hands, relatives and wanderers looking for room and board before hitting the road again.

Hanging high from ceiling beams are dusty ropes and pails of long untouched gadgets. He leaves them that way, just more frozen props from a once active scene. He turns to the front door and steps out slowly into the glare of the real day, heading back toward the house. No guinea hen scolds him, but the sun beats down hard on the button of his gray striped cap. He bows his head, letting the flat bill shade his eyes. It is almost high noon, and it is hard to see the hazy horizon on the other side of this season of retirement.

1977

OUR FARM FROM THE SOUTH

SHE'S STILL PRETTY BUT SHE'S FEELING HER AGE

Rain Storm

It was intermission time. I stepped outside to see how the weather had rearranged our farmyard. Joining my investigation was trooper Heidi-Dog and two unhappy deputy cats. Heidi's white fur was damp and stiff like fine wire; her banana-shaped tail was a truce flag waving in syncopation with the lift-and-shake March of the Saturated Tabbies.

The rain changed the color, scent, size and shape of everything. The haystacks were flattened and sad because their fluffy dance was stifled by the glue of heavy rain. The plowed field was rolling in a rich, deep shade of coal, and the naked walls of the barn were wooden sponges soaking up rain where paint should be. The dented roof of our retired 1950 Ford was a pond of rain-water circled by an orange rusty beach. Lazy leaves were hanging low, too obese to rustle with the frisky breeze. I heard the hum of a motor on the main road as a muddy, gravel-splattered pickup rolled by, incompletely, unleashed from the persistent parachute of summer dust.

Looking up, an ominously silent sky was hanging in layered clumps like wet curdled cottonballs. Wispy strands of a gray-aqua curtain were ready to drop in a spectacular encore. My fingers were numb and my bones quivered (prelude to a shiver). Suddenly, the breeze became ferocious; I turned my back to avoid it, but it was everywhere, it was confused: it

OUR 1950 FORD RESTING WITH DAD'S OLD GRAIN BIN

loved me with hugs, then hated me and shoved me around. Heidi barked to make it behave, the cats abandoned me and I surrendered, allowing it to escort me back to my quarters, knowing that it would patrol my perimeter and catch me on my next escape.

1975

A CAT NAMED SUNSHINE

Sunshine

It scanned
my entire room,
slowly, from one side
to another...
so quietly...
neatly...
with no trace or
proof of its presence
at all
except
for that last warm,
diagonal probe, slowly
squeezing itself closer
and closer into the
furthest wall of the room;
the hard bricks becoming soft,
hungry sponges
absorbing the delicious
light.

(This was my first published poem – written in 1976 and nervously read
to a room of strange faces at the UND Writers Conference in 1978. It
amazed me when so many folks visualized more from my words than
I intended. This must have been the moment when I first realized that
words are tools to carve and create surreal, spiritual visions from what
we take for granted in our day-to-day world.)

COUSIN GINNY

Terry

August 1960 - October 1973

My favorite thing to do was walking. My favorite friend to walk with was my dog, Terry. He grew up with me; he was a gift on my 4th birthday from my cousin Ginny. He was so tiny and shy when we met, and I couldn't convince him to come out from hiding under our wringer washing machine.

Soon, we were best friends. We walked everywhere, through the fields, the pasture, diving for rocks in the creek, and long bike rides. Terry was very brave; I knew nothing bad would happen when he was at my side.

One day, we were about a mile south of home, riding and running, just for the fun of it. I thought I saw something running in the wheat field to my left. I stopped and watched as it continued running, in our direction. The wheat was tall enough to camouflage it, but I was pretty sure it wasn't another dog, and I was puzzled why any strange animal would be running toward us instead of away. Was it brave, crazy, or blind?

Terry started growling and the fur on his back stiffened straight up. He stood between me and the visitor, and I froze. It was a skunk, snarling, wild-eyed, scary. I turned my bike around, pointed north toward home, and called Terry to head out with me, but he didn't follow. I glanced back to see Terry holding his ground, but the skunk zig-zagged past him and was running for me! What!?! What kind of skunk does this!?!

I peddled so fast, I don't think I could do it again if I tried. I prayed that my tires wouldn't hit a loose patch of gravel and send me sprawling down under the feet of this crazy critter. I kept glancing back and saw Terry running in front of the

skunk, like he was trying to herd him away, just like he herds our cows. I knew he was trying to protect me, but who would protect him?

I made it to our barn, dropped the bike, but Terry and the skunk weren't behind me; they weren't around the corner. Where did they go? Terry must have made the skunk hang a left when I hung a right. I didn't dare wander too far from the barn, in case the skunk came tearing out of nowhere after me again. I waited at the barn door. I was worried about Terry getting in a fight with that wild thing. I was worried about rabies.

Finally, at least a half hour later, Terry came around from the north side of the barn, panting and wet with creek water. He wasn't hurt anywhere, no blood or bites or scratches. I asked him what the heck he did with that animal, but he just looked at me like it was simply another normal part of his job as my dog, and he laid down in the tall grass by my feet. The corners of his mouth dimpled up in a little grin, and he looked pleased, and ready for our next adventure.

SHERIE AND JUBILO

Jubilo

There's my guy
with eyes closed tight...
he's so soothing to
my sight.
His purr has ceased.
He's fast asleep...
please, don't disturb
my king of beasts.

SLK 1973

SHERIE AND FRIENDS

Barn Dancing

My circle of stuffed animal friends hugged me in a lazy circle as my daydream bubble bounced between the swirling mobiles on my sky blue ceiling. POP! From a dark corner of the closet, a mean edge of reality snuck up behind me, snagged my breath and popped my pretty balloon. My happy blue walls became a sad shadow. In six months, I must abandon this room; never to know quiet daydream moments here again. Life as I know it will *end*. Man, does that scare me. This room is my friend! It's my security blanket; it lets me be a child, secretly, before I go back out into the strange world and pretend I'm all grown up.

I don't think I'm ready for college. I'd like to spend at least another year here, on my farm. I love this place! There's so many cool memories wrapped around every square inch, every tree, every building and machine. This is where my heart is happy. Home.

The barn…it's my secret haven whenever the house feels too stuffy. So many times, I have climbed the ladder to the upstairs hayloft and perched in the little hay chute doors, overseeing my kingdom of cats and chickens. When I was a little squirt, I practiced my fantasy of being a singer; I grabbed any kind of wooden stick, pretending it was a microphone. Then, I bowed to my audience, consisting of a few scraggly tom cats and maybe a mama cat or two with her small family. Next, I'd swing loudly into the latest pop song I heard on the

SHERIE'S TRACTOR, FACING THE UPSTAIRS
WINDOW OF THE LITTLE BLUE ROOM.

radio. The one that sticks in my mind is "Hello Dolly". Man, did I love that song. Of course, I became a graceful dancer, too. I leaped and swirled around the barn floor, knocking over stools and pails, but it never scared the cats away. They were smart enough to seat themselves in places where my flailing arms and legs couldn't reach. I kept on singing until I ran out of songs or the cats became bored with me and walked out. Then, I moved my act outdoors! It was so much fun, being an entertainer.

Does the dancing have to end, just because I'm growing up? I don't want it to end. I wish I knew what my life will be like...just a little preview, that's all. I don't think I would be so scared, if I could see cats and barn dancing in my future.

Friday, January 18, 1974

VIEW OF EAST PORCH BEHIND WINTER TREES

East Porch

Between my porch and me, a door
of heavy, lonely gloom
protected me from winter chill
but trapped me in a tomb.
Now, with screen door back in place,
the birds, the breeze, the sun
have introduced my sleepy brain
to the equinox of fun.
My porch knows all my secret things…
some are stupid, yes.
I think I'd even be ashamed
if I were to confess.
This porch is such a sturdy friend,
a patient teacher, too.
If I just sit here long enough,
solutions will come through.
It speaks to me about the past;
its floor is warped but strong.
Through lightning storms and twisters
and Torger's silly songs,
cat-nappings and cowboy games,
this porch is family!
Its railings stood in reverence
to prayers on broken knees
offered to the early sun

THE EAST PORCH WAS THE SETTING
FOR EARLY THEATRICAL PRODUCTIONS

both whispered and aloud...
precious moments, humble folks
who now are with the clouds.
My porch has seen the trees, the land
around it grow; improve.
It's reliable and comforting;
a friend that cannot move.

SLK   1973

SHERIE WITH MOM (THELMA), SPRING 2000

Pretty Promises

You always used to watch her. Learning from her every move, the secret to looking happy while smothered in house-wife-unease. Frustration didn't show until little things began doing what they shouldn't. Like hungry cats tipping the cream pail in the barn. You saw her angry foot whip out against the cat's ribs and felt confused. Who needed the sympathy most? You didn't know how to translate her language, so you chose to tip-toe away with the cat. With eyes that spoke and understood and forgave, your cat was your sister, your teacher.

One time, your curious finger pressed too hard on the lever of the box camera. The flash hit the gray metal table-top like spilled water. She pierced into the room and you ran from the scolding words to the cool safety of the barn, the warm fur of true friends. Clever, these comrades distracted you with their antics. This dancing, this sport, this was the antidote for tension.

Now, the years revise your perception. You see her conflict with love versus expectations. You steer away from the traps that chained her to house, church, grocery store. She cannot escape her own contradiction: exhilarated by radio talk-shows and news from the real world while clenching her teeth in stubborn denial ("I don't care to travel to all those fancy places"). You see drops of the hidden dream in her eyes each time she speaks of Mrs. Meldahl, Mrs. Anderson, or anyone with ambition to be free and freedom to use ambition.

And you, daughter, rush for answers through dead-end tunnels. Will you recognize your own exile when it knocks on your door, camouflaged by a cloak of pretty promises and a crooked smile?

1975

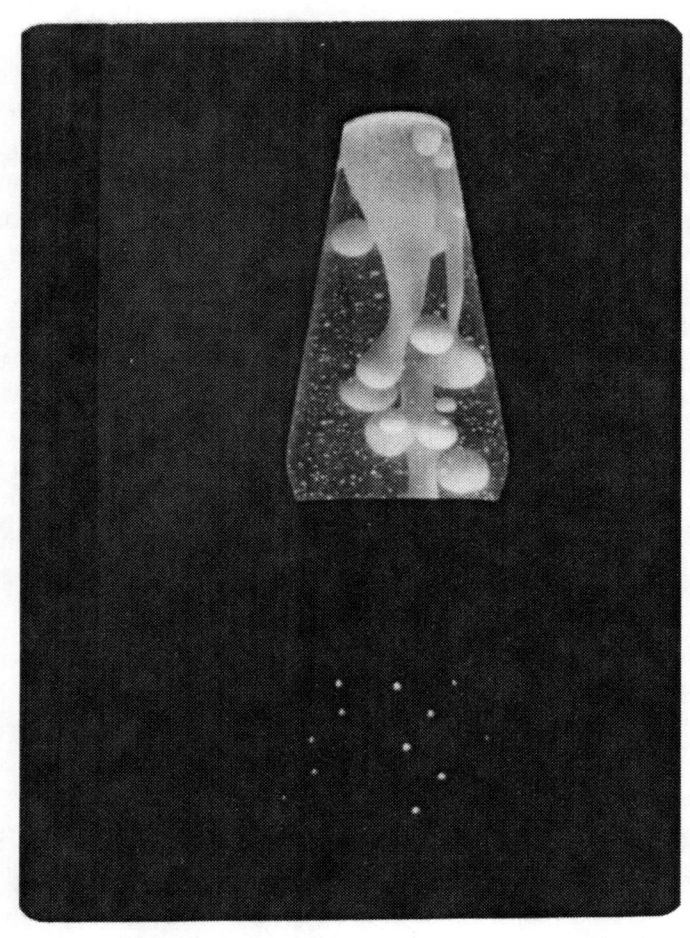

THE DAYDREAM MACHINE

Mister Who

My little heater's running smooth;
my kitty's purr can really soothe.
My floor's not cold; my Fresca is…
my mind just flashed a picture: <u>his</u>.
He's not too ugly, not too cute;
he hardly ever wears a suit.
His smile can fill me with delight
because his teeth are clean and white!
His hair is brown and wavy, too…
his eyes are just a gorgeous blue!
He wears a ring that turns him green;
the car he drives can cause a scene!
He isn't very sexy, but
I don't mind, 'cause he's a nut!
He's not the smug athletic type;
he does his running 'round at night.
He isn't fickle, isn't cruel,
loves his ketchup, hates his school.
He often wears a funny grin
and makes me wonder where he's been!
He's a joker, yes indeed…
he's the kind of guy I need.
And when I find him, if I do,
I'll grab him - *quick* - before you do!

SLK / January 1974

SHERIE'S DAD (JOHN)
FOREVER YOUNG AT HEART!

He is Autumn

The leaves crunch like spilled potato chips under my dad's steady pace. He stops now and then to analyze his work and catch his breath, then shuffles two work-boots forward, bending down slowly from the waist, his knees locked straight, lifting the broad, paint-splattered brush from the gooey red rim of the pail.

His hands, protected by red-freckled canvas gloves, are steady and comforting. I flash back to early childhood moments when all I needed for safety was to feel my hand, so much smaller and smoother, lost inside the warm, protective hug of his hand. These were days when the only entertainment I needed was to stand by his side, my head even with his thigh, and play with his fingers, comparing their size, texture (like warm leather), fingernails (cardboard-thick), and knuckle-joints with my own. I memorized his hands; I knew them better than he did. I've watched them perform: steering a tractor, pounding nails, sawing wood, tying knots, tinkering with cars, and now, painting a wall of the barn.

"Oh, this barn should've been painted many years ago, y'know," he says as the fresh paint soaks into the thirsty old wood. He talks about the crazy paint job many years ago when he set his tallest ladder on top of the haywagon and my sister stood on the highest rung, and still couldn't reach the peak of the wall. He paced and worried and didn't get any work done, so sure she would slip and

crash to the ground. He shook his head, then winked and asked me if I could do that. Even if I wasn't scared of heights, we both knew that he would never let me try. He won't push his luck.

His life has evolved to chores that "should've been done long ago," but "long ago" was a busy time for him, working the farm from sun-up to beyond sun-down. It is awkward, seeing him occupied now with tasks that the women often handled. He was raised under "idleness is sinfulness" and he cannot stop. He requires work, like people require food to survive.

He moves his ladder to a new spot, looks up and scratches his hair under his cap. His eyes are the same color of the sky. This season is quiet and content, settling softly from the busy colors of summer to the sedentary browns, blacks and grays. The lively sounds of chirping birds, buzzing bees and lawnmowers, the clap and clang of working metal, all have drifted into a hibernational hush.

I stir the crunchy brown leaves with my feet. It seems like only yesterday when these leaves were a carnival of life. Too quickly, my dad's summer is over and he is in his late days of fall. What spring season can he look forward to? This land is an old friend who knows his youth, and he will be determined as the prairie wind in sticking around to protect it.

The Lutherans try to give consolation by promising a reunion in the great homestead in the sky. They never paint a clear picture of what it will look like or what will we do there. It seems like there should be something more to heaven than just a painless extension of what we already know.

Farm cats & grandkids love Dad

The Indians trusted the great buffalo and the spirit wolf. Maybe my dad will become the great spirit wind, and someday, when my time comes, I can be the bird who rides with him, performing mystical dances for the lonely souls who look to the sky for answers.

Sherie Lynn Kleven / 1975

DAD, HIS TEAM OF HORSES, AND
BROTHER HERMAN'S KIDS

FROSTY PASTURE SHADOWS
(VIEW FROM OUR WEST KITCHEN WINDOW)

The Lonely Nighthawk

She hovers the blue
where they all used to meet
in the soft days of spring,
in breezes complete
with sunsets that promised
more laughs and new days;
when *hello* meant forever;
they never would stray
from their trees made of ash
and their lake that was golden...
but her youngsters flew far
and her cries couldn't hold them.
Now she hovers and cries
(*they'll return any time!*)
and her eyes aren't as keen
but she'll feel their design,
and her browns will turn green
and the trees will blow kisses
and they'll know that no love
is more brilliant than this is.

So she hovers and cries
through fog and red drought...
she's a friend to the twilight,
a stranger to doubt;
but there's bugs in the sunset
and the Nighthawk is tired;
her flight is a solo -
her song has expired.

(9-5-02 Dedicated to my Mom, Thelma Kleven)

Morning Flight

Rolling rocks. squeaking sand, chattering
seagulls are part of her band.

When last the boxes of music
were played, she ungripped her struggle
and followed the way
lighted by promise,
freedom and love, and she visits me
now as a magnificent dove.

Now when I cry
and raise up my eyes, new
choreography shouts in the skies
a brilliant song
(she's singing along!)
of one life renewed one Sunday
at dawn.

(for Mom, who flew away on Sunday morning 2-9-03)

BABY THELMA (1917) WITH SISTERS
CLARA AND HANNAH

The life of Thelma Helen Berge Kleven

as read at her funeral, February 2003
(followed by a personal farewell letter from daughter to Mom):

Thelma grew up on a farm that was homesteaded in 1886 by her father's widowed mother from Vinje, Norway. Her uncles, aunts, and other elders surrounded her with turn-of-the-century rugged strength and pride. She witnessed, time and time again, that faith and the ties of family loyalty could get you through the hardest times. Her fondest memories were of the folks who still found a way to laugh, to be happy, and to be helpful to others even in their bleakest hours.

It was this philosophy that she carried throughout her life, along with a bottomless cup of anecdotes, dates, and details of our ancestors. Her vivid recollection of all their nuances painted real pictures in our minds, so they came to life again as if they were sitting in the room with us.

She filled our home with nursery rhymes, radio stories, songs and gloxinias. She milked cows who were named after Presidents' wives. She cross-stitched pillowcases and dish towels. She raised baby chicks, nursed sick cats, picked buckets of groundcherries and chokecherries, and watered her garden by bucket brigade. She could prepare any Norwegian recipe you could name. She was a magician in her small kitchen.

NEWLYWEDS JOHNNY + THELMA, 1942

She didn't like to drive, but she would in a pinch. She didn't dance, and drinking, swearing, and card-playing were absolutely forbidden (unless it was a deck of Old Maid). No excuse in the world, no matter how creative, would win her permission to skip church on Sunday. She was in church right up through her last Sunday on this earth.

She happily dedicated a lifetime of hours to Beaver Creek Church: serving at pot lucks, making quilts; she did many inspirational readings in her strong voice which all the hard-of-hearing folks appreciated. She spanned more than 3 decades of planning Sunday school classes and Christmas programs and plays. She never lost the innocence and magic of childhood, and that's why children loved her.

Her trust in God's Word was solid as a rock and she would gladly defend it to anyone who questioned it. She often spoke of the "signs of the times" and how our current events were outlined in Revelations. What would she say about the conflicts we face today?

Friends, neighbors, relatives were drawn to Thelma and Johnny's little farm on the hill because they found friendly conversation and a respite from their chores. The farm was an enchanting escape from the real world. Visitors with tired spirits, broken dreams, or sick house plants, would all leave with their spirits renewed, ready to get back on track (including house plants healed by her green thumb).

Thelma was our cornerstone, the strong one who helped many relatives through their own grieving processes. She left a legacy for us to follow: to be good to each other, patient, forgiving, to help the wanderers find the right path when they're lost, and

The first of many Easter Cakes!

offer warm food and shelter when they're cold.

She loved her life and her family so much that she didn't want to leave us. Her strong heart and spirit persisted long after the rest of her body surrendered. Finally, now she is flying with the wings of eagles, she is running and not weary (Isaiah 40:31). She is renewed in the Light. She is loved FOREVER.

*** written by Sherie Kleven-Jensen, with love for MOM

Dear Mom,

This is a time when words fail me miserably. Your passing has left a hole in my heart the size of the Grand Canyon. No one and nothing can fill it. In the last few years, I came to realize how far we had crossed over that line from being mother & daughter to being friends.

Sundays aren't complete without our marathon phone chats. Without you, music will be flat, spring blossoms will be pale, nursery rhymes will lose their charm, and how will I be able to laugh at the old Norwegian jokes and stories?

What a life! How many pot lucks, Ladies Aid readings, peony bouquets, fat photo albums, silly songs, coloring books, blizzard games, Easter cakes, Christmas secrets, quilting squares, sick cats, old dogs, mean geese, wild pigs, baby calves, healed "owies," wall-rattling wind-storms....you are a bouquet of wonderful, colorful moments....there aren't enough stars in the sky to count all these....

I will miss your spunk. I will miss the times when we read each other's thoughts before a word was spoken, and tears ran down our cheeks from giggling at the same silly thing. Whether in

your apartment or on the farm, times with you were healing and renewing....together, we tried to make sense of the crazy, senseless things in the world and in our family.

Countless nights, we stayed up until the wee hours, recording family history, enjoying the courageous tales of our elders. You said I was too inquisitive, but how could I not be, for within your memory was a treasure of personalities who made us what we are today! I loved to hear every detail over & over, as much as you loved to tell it.

You teased me about taking-in stray cats, but you took in stray people; lost & fearful souls. You built-up their self-confidence, fed them a hearty spiritual meal, and pointed them back out in the right direction.

Now, somehow, life must go on, just as it did when Dad passed away, just as it did for you when you watched your own mom pass away. We are left behind to find our "balance". I don't know where to extend my heart, now that you don't need me anymore. I am lost, but I am happy for you, because now you can do all those things that you've been missing. You can run again, and sing, and garden and laugh and share eternity with the special folks who you have missed so much: your dad, and Clara, and Aunt Catherine, and Uncle Torger, and my dad, and let's not forget your old faithful dog, Walter!

Our last few conversations were so precious. Your body was getting weaker but your spirit was still very strong. The child in you has never died. Oh, how I loved to hear you laugh! Your love for life has always been an inspiration. Your humor was refreshingly innocent, and your unwavering, unquestioning faith

But they that wait
upon the Lord shall
renew their strength;
they shall mount
up with wings as
eagles; they shall run,
and not be weary; and
they shall walk,
and not faint.
Isaiah 40:31

has been the anchor in all our storms!

I will do my best to keep the memories alive, to keep the flame burning. I know there will be many times in my life when I will stop to ask myself, "what would Mom do?". I will try to follow your footsteps of compassion for folks who need help, and I will not lose touch with special relatives. Because of you, Mom, I am who I am, and I will never lose sight of that.

Tusen takk for alt, min mor. Jeg skal husker deg alltid, og nå jeg må bli alene en snill jente, fordi du er engel min som beskytte meg. God Natt, sove godt, drøm behagelig. Jeg elsker deg!!

Din datter,

Sherie

♎

WILD OATS TRAIL
(UND TO SACRAMENTO)

CURIOUSITY

The frozen ground is white,
The winter sky is blue;
Your eyes, they shine like Christmas...
Are you my heart's debut?

December 1976

Restless

The fall afternoon sunshine was tempting her fidgety mood. Surrounded by a snarl of menacing textbooks, she sat in yoga folds on the corner of her bed, head bent and forehead creased. Holding a highlighter over unworthy words, her hand was cuffed and decorated with silver jewelry. Her free hand twittered about, drumming fingers to the beat in her head or flying up to twirl and untangle the flattened curls in her shoulder-length hair. Her sighs were in harmony with the breeze, sneaking in through the green stripe curtains.

Outside her window, action filled the still world like jumping notes bringing life to an empty score sheet. The background browns of grass, balding trees and brick buildings were decorated with wheels and wings and weightless leaves. Shades of a scarlet sunset swerved between the feet of studious warriors, charging through the chilly edge of autumn.

She dropped her notebooks like an avalanche, unfolding her dance legs and spiraling up in a long stretch. Drawing angel wings in the air, she greeted the mirror, grabbed her keys and sauntered in five easy steps toward the door. With an elaborate flick of the wrist, proclaiming power over the doorknob, she tossed blonde sparks into the rejected room and set out to conquer her own sliver of wilderness.

1976

Airman of Choice

I write your name
because it is the
closest I can be
with you now.
I write it slowly,
languishing over each
letter, caressing
the curves
and angles.
The letters are
beautiful and sad.
I wish our moments
could be as smooth
and poetic
as my pen.
I run the tip of my finger
over your name,

hoping that
someday, you will
trust me,
touch me,
discover me,
show me your
wounded, hidden corners.
Please! You are
my muse…
let me
be your poet.

1976

Campus 1975

Where did we all begin, now swarming like working bees inside this academic hive? Big-name stars in family photo-albums, our importance has faded here. Never as precious as they saw us, bouncing on their bony, loving knees, the world blends us into one.

It doesn't matter whether we come from the Emerald City or the wrong side of the tracks. Teachers, with a sweeping gaze, look on us like sky-gazers on a starry night (notice the bright ones). I look around and see that I am just another blur in the galaxy.

It's winter again and we wonder about our goals. Doubts grow as temperatures drop and we slide through the icy days, hoping the slick hand of Fate may gently crash us into a comfortable career. I have only the sturdy handle of friendship to grip and stop the slip into a cold drift of nowhere; this is my beacon, my comfort. I will survive this oblivion.

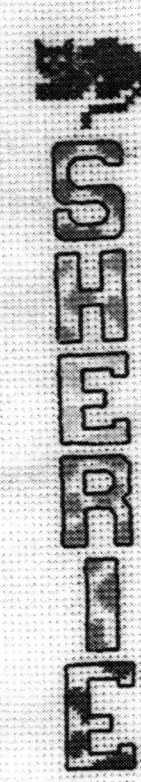

Nicknames

Nicknames sure are
weird, you know?
They're goofy as a
curly toe.
Did Louie, McHenry,
Fritz and Boone
step off the page
of a Sunday cartoon?
Shatzi, Stub, T-Bone,
Cornelius and Rickster, too
seem to have much more fun
than just plain Bob or Sue.
My cat's Mr. Tux,
my car is Blue Pea,
but I'm pretty boring:
I'm only known as me.
A Rosey or a Spacey or
a Bongo would be fine...
but with my darn luck...
they'll call me Gooberstein.

1973

Symphony

Soft, sweet notes flow through the silver wand of a simple, slender, black gift of diversion. Like the scent of spring lilacs, the notes fill the air around me, invading my inner privacy, monopolizing all emotions with a steady, hypnotic rhythm.

Suddenly, like the rushed breeze before a storm, the beat becomes animated and the notes rise, almost frantically, stirring the depths of my soul. Resonating, alive, the music resides within me, holding me in inspired suspension, making me wait, breathlessly, like a fan at the Kentucky Derby, wondering which horse will burst through the finish line into the wild shower of flowers and pandemonium.

Crescendo! The notes are violent, frightening, exhilarating. My heart gasps as it feels the pinnacle of passion; strings and flutes are dizzied while drums celebrate the lofty panorama. Hovering, the melody allows me to savor this moment...and I relax into the soothing breath of murmuring woodwinds. The notes float down...down...settling into tranquility, restfulness, like falling upon a soft bed at the end of an exhausting day.

Languishing under a golden sunset, the song fades, gently, regretfully, in a long and sad goodbye.

October 1974

Opaque Fingertips

Monotone workday
fades
to your steps,
composing me.
Your keys
release the orphaned
colors and
you stir me with a hug
and
our auras play on
to a midnight crescendo,
saturating
the pale moon in a
crimson moment.
Your opaque fingertips
stroke me into
melodic folds,
falling into a
hushed
corner of night,
and we rest
in lazy measures
toward
the rising lavender
light.

TRUE LOVE

HOT DAY

Only flies move
in this room.
Pools of weariness
slump in each chair
with legs and arms
dripping off the edges
to idle islands
of ashtrays and footrests.
Minds numb
to the Fahrenheit attack
as eyes lock
their lashes together
and sweat-beads on
tense foreheads
spell out
Do Not Disturb.

SLK
UND study hall
1976

KNOT NOW

Slippery knot
        and sweaty palms
        struggle
    through the dusk
                for freedom
                for possession
and unraveled
        escape is in each thread
        from the gnarled
                core, clawed by raw
and ravenous fingers.
        Myriad shadows
                sucked from the tenacious twine are
raped
        slowly
                by the sun, soothing
hideous knuckles.
        The yawning grip stretches into
        new strategy,
                        and the knot cowers
toward daylight just
                smaller than itself.

3-15-85

Midnight Spoon

Ice cream loses
its firm, pretty shape
and hides
in the bottom
of my bowl
just as
all hopes sink
under my
overcooked
stew of delusions.

Chocolate syrup
smothers but
does not destroy
the vanilla.
Suspicion
mutates love.

It's good to have a dog to keep you warm
(Sherie & Terry 1969)

The soft underbelly
of my soul is
branded
and skewered
by a hot blade of
arrogance.

My frozen friend
curls up and
spoons me, gently
licking my
tortured heart.

1977

Now

Frosted islands
of crunch
are caught
inside
blue palms,
and morning
winds
bite
like hungry
flies
as woolen
clouds
scent
the air of
autumn's exit.

SLK
October 1977

Blue Eyes

Like a twizzling comet
to a humble
tumbleweed, he is,
or the sparkle of Christmas
to a tedious Monday,
he is.
Like childhood in my
lifetime and friendship in
loneliness, he is.
A wink from his blue eyes
satisfies my soul
like hamburger in
starvation or
Southern Comfort
on a Saturday night,
causing rushed color
to my cheeks; he
completes my day.

1976

AAAIIIYYYEEEEEOUWOOOOO !!

My mind, my heart, my gut
quiver and shiver
as his name and face and voice
pour in, around, and through me,
filling me from fingertips to toes.
He's in my ears and nose
and my hair, which he touched, and
my nails, which we wrestled and wrecked,
and my shoulders, which he hugged.
He's causing ulcers, flunked tests,
and smokin' sneakers.
He's giving me an insane laugh and
worried friends now
looking to rent a straight-jacket
for their safety from my fits.
He leaves for Alaska Thursday...
a month gone, will I live that long?
I should tell him; how do I tell him?
I am filled with him and there's more
him coming in and
the scotch-tape and stitches will
break and split me open and
spill my churned feelings
everywhere!
(Hope he's in the everywhere then.)   (1976)

COUSIN BURKLEY IN SHERIE'S
FIRST BLUE CAR

Flying Low
(my Blue Pea and me - 1973)

My Maverick takes me
where I want, and often,
where I don't.
People tell me not
to drive, but I can't stop...
I won't!

Actually, when I began,
I was not
so frightening...
but then I scratched
a reckless itch
and my Maverick
grew wings!

With age and some
reluctant smarts,
I've calmed down a bit...
but Blue Pea is my
juvenile,
revved-up
and full of spit!

Two LeadFoots (Sherie & Lisa) get smart
with alternative forms of travel

The wonder of this all,
you see (and this
is *really weird*), is
that this car
is never hurt (by now,
it should be
smeared).

My crazy little monster
cannot resist
the ditch...
but I do wish it would
warn me, please...
I'm developing a twitch.

Fallen Star

Through the foreign night,
my heart floated
down
      down
            down
like the homeless flicker
from a forlorn star
rejected by
heaven.

Today I walk
on the cold slab of logic.
      Burned
from the feast of fireworks,
my tired eyes have
      spiraled
back to the reliable
flavors found around
      five-foot-five.

Neutered,
the butterfly riot has
yielded its corners of
      carnage,
      leaving room
for a reunion with food.

Steady now,
      unbroken,
I see how it is with him.

Still, I wait to see him again.

1977

139

Forbunds #314

Down
and out
beyond the pale
and wrinkled
lamp shade,
an empty alley
holds
faded
plastic
flowers
for no one.

In
and around,
protests race
the
rising pulse
while
Karl Johan
turns his back.

Scowling
and sighing,
phony curtains
wave
but
do not applaud
the
hard lesson,
pushing Mom's prayers
into a
pile of dust
on the worried floor.

June 1978

The Ultimate Trap

She's
with nature, you know.
Spits
of thorns from the
rosebush are a laugh to those
who pilfer
the beauty
each season and the newly
purged
tide must
always
return to kick-out more garbage
after
sweating
to be itself.
The goldfish turns
gray
when pre-orgasmic nostrils and
bars
of whiskers fill the bowl's neck....and
she
loves him again...his
entrance will
destroy or toy with her
essence.
Ultimate trust?
Naturally.

9-28-85

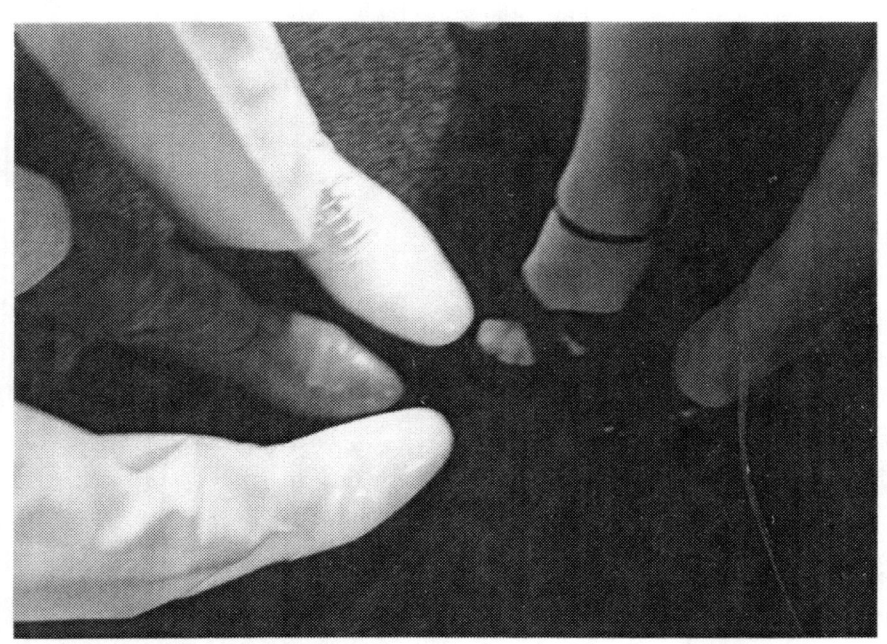

Ravenous Vacuum

You spread me thin
like a carpet
and then
gather my threads
into patches of
piles.
There. You've got me
under your feet
and your toes
wriggle
happily through
the labels.
You can't take me
as a tweed.
If I were a
Calico cat,
you'd dye my
fur so I'd be
simpler
to see.
No. You push

yourself in
to where I want you
out, like an
eyeball
in a keyhole,
you take
what I won't give
and see it
all
in black
and white.

Sherie L. Kleven-almost-no-Payne 1983

Wild Oats

The time begins as
      heated flowers pull
      her from his
      obstinate door to a sigh and
      a crystalline bag spilling
                traces
        of metamorphosis.
      Her soles
          crush
          the naked layers
    of unholy shale,
          stuttering
            through chiseled air
     to meet a
            reckless scent kissing her breath as she
                              speeds
Flashing lights weep, and   into
wheels hold her near in a dance   delirium.
on flirtatious streets

toward an angular flight which
    pales
    her florid release.
                A slap
       of incredulous air spins her into suspicion. She
discards
her
deviance
       in the fresh tracks of the dream....
  she...has
          lost
     her fine jeweled bag
and stumbles to his
open door
with only a paper sack filled
with dead marigolds.

08/04/84

KEVIN AND SONS (JASSEN, ERICK)
AT CASTLE ROCK CAVES

♎

HIDING IN THE WOODS
(HEALED, CONCEALED, REVEALED)

What Is It?

Through and through the needle's eye,
over the clock and 'round the sky...
kissing frogs and rabbits feet
with dandelions curled and sweet,
it rides the wind to northern star,
out of reach but not too far.
In whispered wait for sunrise dance,
it chaperones the child named "Chance".

February 22, 2002 (chasing the elusive truth)

Green-Tail Cat

Laughing eyes fold under
the long tale of a
heavy cloak
which does not warm,
tugs at our struggles and
compresses Our Confusion into shapes
which can never contain It.
We are lost at the intersection
of Desire and Disaster, searching for
reassurance that our climb is worth
the time.
Sweet memories of home
swallow our scars
and form a mirage that we cannot catch
and cannot abandon.
Through my tears, I smell my father's
corduroy fields and I see my mom's green-tailed
cat in her window with a silly sign
"I Wuv You Madly." He is watching
the harmless farm shadows dancing
under our moon on a pole.
I close my eyes and stretch high
for a hug

from an ancient wind...
I can almost taste how it feels
to relax and heal
when the Black Tale
whips my wrists and
knots them to my ankles,
buckling ribs and rubbing my nose
in the furrows of my fabrications
and dusty tales of days wasted
by haste
and stranded conversations in
the ditches with angry,
homeless kisses nipping at the heels
of useless excuses.
My illusion is consumed.
Deprived of dancing, I am only
a stone
with a hardening heart and petrified
eyes, fixed on a funny
green tail that finally turns
gray, and fades.

April 2004

A stick poem, about a stick all alone:

Once, a tree that was kind
to all of its guests -
offered birdsong and shade
and made no requests -
was severed and suddenly
orphans were strewn
from their mother, the
only source of their bloom.
Paralyzed cries
under weight of the tread,
the sad orphan stick
knew he soon would be dead...
but a curious boy
rescued him from the trail,
named him after a ship and
set him to sail
where he danced with the water
in freedom from harm
until captured and choked
by algae's green arm.
A sweet yellow lab
plucked him out like a frog,
and the stick died in honor,
loved by a dog.   2-5-03

SWEET BUDDY

BUDDY

October 6, 2001 – March 6, 2002

A small life: an ornament
rolling through a holiday in time -
an introduction from a visitor
to strange laughter that was mine!

Softly curious, his halo eyes
wondered often at the sky...
was it birds or cruel angels
arranging his goodbye?

These sorry hands caressed him,
pruned shadows from the sun,
but his dance was with calamity;
he was the chosen one.

Kidnapped by a twist of fate;
he saw no summer, saw no spring.
I *hate* Divine Conspiracy
for this atrocious sting!

A dimple in the face of time;
when will I be consoled?
Love is more enormous with
only remnants left to hold.

No morning bird that I can hear,
no light that I can see
will usher him through starry fields
and sweet umami trees.

Pierced, in stumbling, sightless search
through grim and lonely night,
I won't be soothed until I find
the ghost of all that's right.

Raven Rock

Quail on branches
tuck inside early morning
blankets of sun; their breasts glow
as the ascension escapes the sleepers
and keepers of poly-polymers.

Whitetail dad distracts the dogs
while fawn and mom find a fine
dessert of apples splashed
with birdbath.

Kaleidoscopic hummers spin
around a fresh gift of wine from
the blonde human who struggles
toward their magic as
demanding demons steal her away.
Brown wet nose nudges her
elbow, begs her to stretch and play...
and for a second, she sees
an escape in Simba's eyes and
through her soul....

Later, trudging home, she hears the
whispered worries of horizontal maples
rolling in the strange asphalt breeze.
She sighs and bows her head from
their 4WD coffin, feeling like a sunflower
who lost the sky.

She carries her cares to
her golden friend on the hill, waiting
and happy the hunt filled her
pockets with more biscuits than coins.

Dropping wristwatch and worries, she
frees her toes and grabs Simba's
tail away from the darkness of day
through dragonfly shadows and fossils
of fox claws. On the great rock ladder to
Methuselah tree, Simba sniffs,
"What's this?" pivoting over a mottled
feather with stories to tell...
"It's a magical feather, Simba, see...
ssshh..." they study it nose-to-nose and
(whoosh!) their breath revives
the echoed flutters
of a flight beyond their eyes...

Smiling, Simba pilots the feather to the
top of Raven rock, just as Methuselah
catches the sun in a cradle draped
in melting light;
the twilight bouquet
explodes and absorbs the dregs
of the day.

Chewing on chokecherries in
moondust meringue, they
thank Raven rock
and wish that this moment
could be their domain.

August 2001

Mizaru's Magic Paint

Tomorrow
I will wear sunset colors.
In pyro-peach, baby
blue and taziac teal,
I will stand
proud like that tree
sporting a
sunray bowtie
for his date with the
ballerina of the branches.

I'll pretend I'm the wind,
who's not choosy
about his dance partners.
I will memorize
the lyrics of the leaves
and hold them close
like a friend.

The Dipper tonight
looks dapper as it was
when I played
with Mizaru, Mazaru,
and Mikazaru, painting
tree rings to tally
the stars.

I abandoned them
and lost what counts
and learned to kiss
my pain,
but tomorrow,
I will create a
meadowlark sunrise
with Mizaru's magic paint,
and I will hug
fragile moments
before they shatter
like dropped
dreams at dawn,
and hitch
my wagon to
the tail of Orion's belt.

3-8-03

Pale Footsteps

You threw my flowers in
the blender and chewed
your charm down to
jagged horns
that bruise our blessings.
The InnoScents are contaminated
by your fumes, and I
can barely keep my head above
the ruins.
With dumb luck or
prayer, a pocket of clean air
pulls me toward a
tunnel with no light. I
measure my stumbling by
the groans of doleful creatures
in the grip
of wrong turns.

Tracking my pale footsteps
through your desert
of unsettling dust
will only lead to a trail of
splintered dreams and
my shredded subscription
to your Storm of the Month.   (February 2004)

173

The Dragon

A little girl
near the edge
thought
she saw a pretty boy and
thought
she saw him smile with a curious
orange glow, so she tip-toed closer
but he vanished in a snuff.

She looked around
and only saw the face
of a cast iron stove.
Never before
knowing this kind of warm,
she removed her pretty clothes
and climbed naked
toward the smile in the
flickering flames as the door
closed behind her
and the stove swallowed, dropped its mask,

turned and lifted
a scurrilous shadow over the
open field of short time
where eyes of white birthdays
cannot see dragons.

They found her clothes curled
around a cold rock
on the other side of hope,
and never saw the little girl again.

1-5-03

Chewy Books

Rain
    dropped
        like pennies
in dancing islands
    around Roscoe's feet,
ornaments to his trail
like the nursing sprigs
to Mother Spruce.
    The sun and his smile
    came out curly,
        rounding
the trees and
    shuffling the shadows
of squirrels and birds.
Finding a quirky piece of dirt,
    he stopped
    to chew on a tale
    wrapped-up in a stick,
and his eyes filled with
shiny apples and ladybugs.
    With a playful roar

R-R-ROSCOE THE CHARMER

and a strange
            little twist,
    he tucked a morsel of the
            moment
            under his chin
and carried it home for dessert.
        The moss joined in wet applause
        as he galloped
            just in time
to hear the first purring from
            dark corners
        circling her slumber.
        He found
        a steak of words that tasted
        like old sticks with flakes
            and curled-up
        to guard her chamber,
            waiting for her face to rise,
        anxious
        to show her
        how to consume books
            instead of worries.

October 6, 2002

Sabrina

My brave little dot,
you punctuate shadows
and underline
the wings of the owl.
Pouncing through hidden passages,
you drop gifts of fun inflections at
the door of my flattened clichés.
I awake to find you purring,
pondering the jewels
of the morning sun.
Swish! Your whiskers erase
a dangling dream
and you greet me
with italicized eyes.
Up! Up! Marking double-exclamations
in the vertical air,
you dance in new dialects, with
tail-twitching symbols of
Celtic slang; your paws
are parentheses
to my stuttering ankles.

When I leave, you protest in
BOLD LETTERS but I
return to forgiveness in
fluttering meows and
curious circles.
Stalking...
with heroic rhythm...
you exhaust my bag of worries,
boxing it around
like a bug.
In the last margin of twilight,
with a lingering stretch, you pull
my fragments together,
close one eye and
tuck yourself into a sleepy comma
around my ear.

June '05

Millennium Spring

Coyote camps and frog ponds deep
sing loud to end spring's time to sleep.
Yellow petals light the trail
of melting snow and sleeping snail.
Pools of melted caramel sun
transform the sad brown eyes of one
who finally sees the swallow's white
like stars and angels: end the night!!
Frolicking colors, splashing bouquets
escape from tombs eclipsed in grays.
Forget the screen's hypnotic drone;
four walls no longer feel like home…
my soul must ride the virgin breeze,
kiss mossy fingers hugging trees
and rocks with muddy faces sweet;
let dancing rainbows find my feet!

3/18/00

Willow in Winter

5-28-00

She weeds in the snow (what do calendars know)
while the mission bells die 30 days from July.

She guards the mundane at age 43;
her songs have no voice,
her moments, no choice,
but her clocks and her chores all agree.

The jewels that count are tucked far away:
Mom tethered to sleep
near Valhalla the deep...
pale strangers will roll her that way...

Oslovian sister with man who won't sleep
fills hollow dreams,
hides monthly screams...
and he calls her "Be Little Bo-Peep".

The span of her youth cannot double it's time:
stretching will fail,
glow becomes stale,
no adventure caressing her rhyme.

Songbirds are preachers to souls in distress;
wings cannot choke,
magic's no joke
to the winds rearranging the west.

Willows must bend and dance with the sky;
woman must dare
to *laugh*, not compare -
to defy all the drones who comply.

The brave little swallows fly under the moon
and care nothing about our winter in June.

Aurora, Impaled

A pink flannel child with no one to kiss;
a wandering soul without family to miss…
fireflies paled by a world without night
and a puppy's lost smile for a face without sight…
the last shooting star with no one to wish;
a gray ocean barren of golden starfish…
a hug of forgiveness for someone not home;
dried kisses that crumble, drift over old bones…
the last haunting note that can't find a tear;
hummingbirds trapped in windowless fear;
a discarded companion who patiently waits
while a clipped and caged dove mourns her own fate.

A young penguin hatched in a nest with no mom;
a fairy tale sunset, after the bomb.
A dreamer at dawn on the day it all ends…
a heaven that's void of all our old friends…
an old man who's lost the face of his bride;
Quixote's friend Sancho when knightly tales died…
the unfortunate shamrock in withering light;
the ghosts of Galapagos haunting the night…
dark churches, shrouded in labyrinth locks
as men and their money begin to have talks:
"Subterranean arks for the last of each breed!
We'll build them and spaceships and save our own seed!"

…the last seal ball harvest, the last elephant tusk;
the last owl to cry as the moon shrivels to dust…
on the corpses of forests, falls Aurora, impaled,
with no poet to write about paradise failed.

June 30, 2001

One Last Walk

ToFisk (a.k.a. ToCat, ToFur, To-Baby, To-Meister, Toadstool, To-To-Too) was born in Citrus Heights, CA. Her mother was a beautiful white princess, and the lady of the house was a customer on Sherie's Avon route. ToFisk left her mother and her little black freckled brother when she was 6 weeks old. Sherie was her new mom now.

ToFisk means "two-fish" in Norwegian. She was born on the 22nd of the month under the sign of Pisces. What a relief that they didn't name her "blå blomster" because of her sapphire eyes!

She liked her new home with green shag carpet, big shady trees to hide in and a friendly uncle-cat named Greedy-Gut who watched over her. She made a cozy bed inside her mom's shoes until, for some reason, they shrunk and she couldn't squeeze inside anymore.

Her mom took her for rides around town in a little red car. ToCat loved to stretch in the sun under the back window, and when they stopped at a drive-through, she celebrated her moment in the spotlight; how easy it was to charm these strangers with a fluff of her tail and a flash of blue eyes!

She was young, but she knew what play-fighting was. Her mom and the man of the house were not play-fighting. They didn't like each other anymore, so she had to leave Greedy-Gut to be with her mom in a very scary room, way up high, with loud engines outside, slamming doors below, and hot, so hot. She missed her shady trees. She didn't like the armies of bugs that came out at night. Each day when her mom came home to put ice cubes in the fish tank, ToFisk came out of hiding, hoping that mom would smile again and take her for a ride, far, far away. But then the walls would rattle and scare her back under the bed.

GREEDY GUT!

She knew the signs: boxes, suitcases, friends coming in and out and...wow, mom was smiling again! What a happy day it was when she ran through the rooms of her new house! A fidgety old lady with big noisy birds lived next door. That was fine with ToCat; big birds didn't scare her. She loved the huge yard! The dog across the street tried to chase her, but mom always stepped in the way to protect her.

A couple years passed; she knew the noisy peacocks by name, and a new man came to visit mom. She liked him; she sat in his lap (an honor she gave to no one but mom), and mom was laughing and singing. This was a good sign; each time he visited, ToCat hoped he would stay and live with them.

One day, mom and this man were wrestling on the floor and even though mom was laughing, ToCat wasn't sure this was safe. She jumped on top of him and bit his arm, just hard enough to stop and warn him that she was there to protect mom. He laughed, but she knew she earned his respect that day.

Uh-oh. There were the boxes, the suitcases, the friends in and out, the rooms getting bigger and bigger. Good-bye, big birds, good-bye, fidgety lady. ToCat went for a lo-o-ong ride with mom; she worried that it would never end and they would ride forever. The air smelled different: wet? Yes, it was wet air - with a hint of fish?

Finally, her mom stopped the car and carried her to a green house. There was a big red bush by the front door; ToCat liked that - she could see many hiding places in those branches. The man who made mom laugh was there, too. His name was Kevin. Mom let her investigate the house and then she saw the big back yard! Ahhh, this was a good playground; Greedy-Gut would have loved it. Mom told her that she was a Redwood City kitty now, and that sounded okay to ToCat.

KEVIN AND THE TO-MEISTER

Searching for Garfield!

When mom and Kevin spent a weekend in the cabin in the woods, ToCat came along. The giant trees were filled with the scent of something big and wild. ToCat loved it and feared it at the same time; she stayed close to mom.

Back home, she made friends with the neighbors except the mean lady who always yelled at her. Mom started driving a big yellow bus, and ToCat loved to run up to the swinging glass doors to greet her. One time, she hopped inside to look around, but she was overwhelmed by the noisy engine and the aromas of so many different people.

Cardboard boxes and tape, again!!??! Now where were they going? What a relief when mom took her out of the car after driving only a few minutes. ToCat found herself in the biggest playground of all time! This house was where she discovered "UP." Upstairs, up on the roof, into the attic, down to the basement, back to the garden, through the hedge; ToCat was thoroughly entertained and she hoped they would stay here forever!

An old gentleman lived downstairs with a very tiny lady. He made funny noises but she never said a word; she paced a lot, going nowhere. ToCat watched her mom and Kevin when they washed and dressed and fed food to this lady. She was so restless, they learned to tuck her in with special sheets so she wouldn't fall out of bed at night.

One night, ToCat followed mom when she checked-in on the tiny woman who never spoke. What a surprise when she lifted her head and said, "Hi Kitty!" The next day, a round man in black robes came to say strange words over the tiny lady and she was not restless anymore. Serious, silent people carried her out of the house the next morning while the old gentleman cried.

They stayed there for many years, and ToCat knew every nook and cranny of the estate. She loved to sneak out through the dormer window and climb on to the roof where she sat for hours, even with the tree tops, watching the world below.

ToCat was 10 years old when she heard her mom and Kevin talk about having their own house, somewhere else. ToCat thought *this* was her own house; doesn't living in it make it your own? People have confusing rules.

Many, many cardboard boxes were packed and the rooms began to get bigger. Kevin disappeared first, leaving mom behind long enough for ToCat to think that maybe they weren't leaving after all. But then the day came when everything disappeared into the boxes. Mom was crying a lot; she didn't want to leave? This worried ToCat, and when mom put her in the cat carrier, she worried even more because it looked like a long trip. And it was.

Days later, they pulled in to a place that smelled like the cabin in the woods, only different. Mom carried ToCat into a brown house and let her run. Ya-hoo! Free at last! There was a lot to investigate here, she could see, and mom reassured her that this was the last time they would move.

Winters were long and cold and white, but ToCat was happy as long as mom and Kevin fed wood into the big black stove. Springtime and summer were the happiest times. Mom had many gardens outside and ToCat followed her around to supervise the worm and weed digging. On sunny afternoons, mom would read a book next to the flowers by the driveway and ToCat tucked herself into tufts of grass for a nap.

After a life of being chased by dogs, ToCat learned to live with them when she was 12 years old. The first puppy was Ruby and then Simba joined the family. Without knowing it, ToCat tantalized these puppies with her irresistibly fluffy tail. In time, mom convinced the newcomers that it was not okay to chase the kitty. Eventually, a miracle happened as ToCat accepted these two dogs as her friends. When mom took a walk, ToCat, Ruby and Simba would follow. At each stop, ToCat weaved herself in and out of Simba's legs, rubbing her back on Simba's belly. Ruby's legs were too short for this.

They all learned to speak the same language. When mom whistled, ToCat and the dogs would come running. When the music was on, they each brought their own unique dance steps to the floor around mom's feet. When a lightning storm rolled in, they all hid on the same side of the bed. Mom's can opener was a happy sound, and ToCat knew she was a lucky girl when mom crunched up bits of cabbage with her food. Yum!

Sweet 16 wasn't so sweet for ToCat. She had a good appetite but she was losing weight. By the time she turned 17 in February 1999, only her tail and her big blue eyes were their normal size. She was shrinking, and it took longer to warm up and to stretch and move. Mom's doctor gave her some advice and mom seemed to spend more time than usual with her in the sunny spot by the driveway. ToCat wanted to walk with mom and the dogs, but she was so tired.

One warm August Sunday, while sitting in the sun with mom, ToCat stood up and walked down the driveway because she thought someone had called her. After a few paces, she stopped, turned and looked back at mom who was still sitting in the lawn chair. This wasn't right. ToCat never went on walks without mom; what was she doing? She turned in her tired, unbalanced way, and came back to sit with mom. Not long later, ToCat stood up again, hearing the same call to start walking. Again, she turned to see mom watching her. Mom said, "Where are you going, little one?" This was strange; mom always knew where their trips would take them; why didn't mom know about this one? ToCat had a feeling she was supposed to go somewhere, but she didn't want to leave mom, so she made herself come back.

The next morning when mom found her body in a cold little curl, ToCat had succumbed to the call and set out alone on a new journey, without cardboard boxes, suitcases, or mom.

Sleeping Sapphire Eyes

For ToFisk - my faithful white shadow:
February 22, 1982 - August 9, 1999

How will I enjoy the beauty of lillies
without To-Cat posed in their shade?

How can trees kiss the blue souls above
as the season trades swallows for wasps?

The hummingbird's dance in the rainbow spritz
is a dream as the drops turn to dust....

And who will catch the red ball of summer as it
falls brown under pigskin parades?

My sighs will not turn the sands back to color
and my tears will not water the birds...

Alone with the sad, smoking forest,
I trace the footprints of To-Cat's goodbye....

(ToBaby, I am so sorry. I know you really wanted me
to go with you on one last walk...)

THE LAST WOLF

In a world where no one knows his name,
he waits....and worries...what are these
icey blue teeth that betray the face of
an old sweet breeze? Who is this alien rain,
spitting and forgetting a summer caress?
He offers a splintered song
that is met only by hurling remnants of
a shredded season.

When did the chatter of friends become
ominous calls to follow the last
lonely owl..."Fall, fall, fall away
from your hollowed home..."
Where, where is that golden memory
that made him stay? Is it the strange,
impaled corpse, fallen from a hot grip to the
porcupine snow?

The rain flies like a witch on an icicle stick, shrieking and
spitting shrapnel on the playground of shoots,
damming the portals and prayers of all
evicted colors.
Cornered by this restless cauldron,
his ragged blue eyes search

for a sliver of moon to cut
the black mist...

*(His last dream cradles him in a warm, pink light, lifting him
through renewed skies to a jeweled spectrum of familiar
voices,
showering their seeds on the barren Pyrenees...)*

The cackles have sliced his veins and soon he will
fall, under strange tearless skies, without the owl's call.

01/01/01

HUSHED LITTLE HOLOCAUST

You stripped a proud mother of
nine jewels of promise, soiling their
threshold of life with the stench
of your footsteps.
Expelled to a cruel tomb, their
tangled cries congealed with your
slimy prints, marking
the scene of your sin.
If wishes could spit, the moon would
flood your feculent spine from this
depleted planet...instead,
your malignant spoor will be
probed and prosecuted by Orion
and his omnipotent host.
At the inquest of your hushed
little holocaust, may the howls of
the muted forever sever
your vile supplications to the
God you have shamed.

1-10-01
(published in the Letters-to-the-Editor section of
the Spokesman Review, addressed to the
anonymous monster who dumped nine living,
newborn puppies in a dumpster)

A Happy Slice of Air

With eloquence and whimsy,
they are my sunrise dance:
a carnival of brilliance,
a song of happenstance.

A newborn heir to rainbows
at the pinnacle of flight
is curious and well-equipped
and unrestrained by fright.

His entourage of clever wings
teach basic pirouettes...
while lowly leghorn worries
over wishbones captured yet.

Spinning, tumbling, fluttering
into luminous ascent;
they tease me and they leave me
in my lumbering lament.

The high celestial language
of lost balloons and rhymes
translated by the chuckling creeks
untangles them from time.

They see the tool that circles crops
(it's where the angels play),
they hear the harmony of souls
embraced in star bouquets.

From dirigibles to dragonflies,
to Armstrong's lunar call...
all flights excite and end like dreams:
epiphanies for large and small.

Empty sky. Silent tree.
Breathless serendipity!

8-13-00

(Amelia's propellor
took a happy slice of air
and found a home not flattened
by inconsequential care...)

Quiet Treasure

The sun hit her back as she
faced the flattened shadows of
her cardboard ecstasy.
The clock struck 1:00 and the world
inverted:
embers of an old voice were scooped and kindled
by a wily wind spilling
her sequestered treasures in
a storm of orbiting auras.
Brilliant red oaks whispered: "This way, this way, this way..."
and she followed their
applause of the new light.
Fences and pretenses became spittle on the vine that
sprouted
into a blazing trail, lifting her to a curious
chorus of cats with wings and
bears with rings around a freshly star-kissed moon.
The remnants of her ascent were softly
sifted and tucked
with the whisps and whiskers of
quiet treasures,
only to be seen
when sweetpeas chatter
and butterflies sing to the sun.

October 8, 2000 (turning 44)

Twisted Teeth

Her spirit, chewed-up by
dubious debts, was spit back
out as a doleful dram
of the person
she planned to be.
She boggled through
wambling paths of
twisted teeth to a dead-end
where the wind
whistled for her to jump.
One look back
at the spindly smiles
who directed her daze,
and she laughed them off
like a spring redwing
untethered
by time or whimsical weather.
She stepped out
with the guilty foot
that once stumbled twice
upon the same stone
and discovered how to walk,
sure as that turtle
on the fencepost.

She screwed her toes on straight
and followed
the glitter of the visitor
leading her dreams,
away from the safety mist
in her mother's eyes and into
a blushing twilight to
mate with Darkness
in a dance that celebrates
Light.
They brushed the moonlight
off her muffs and mittens, and
every tooth she lost along the way
lit up in a mysterious
script to her very own play.

9-1-02

3 NOSES!

Broken Toys

(10-23-02)

She cleans because they would be shocked
at her mess, if she were to die today.
The reindeer have danced through her old
rhubarb patch and now they invite her away
from the hurt that's her present on her birthday
that's not, from the boy who broke all her toys.

While the magpies are restlessly showing her how
to be splashy and trashy with noise,
3 noses who velcroed their steps to her heart
lead her out to the sun-painted moon
where their auras *just miss* a rescuing kiss
speeding by in terrestrial tune.

The mushrooms are too embarrassed to look
and the old trees are moaning her name...
the young trees are angry and slapping her face
as she turns back to the same way she came!
Tears are the trophy of invisible ghosts
whispering lists of what's wrong.
The cliffs that were bookends hugging her hope,
sadly seal up the tomb of her song.

It's midnight, the height of her own Pleiades
when untethered shadows consume what they seized.

Reid Frojen - Sharon H.S. Class of '74

Sliding

Her knuckles are
white as the snow
on her rainbow
and her grip slips.
She slides down the purple band
and turns
to throw me a gift:
her smile, exuberant,
blooming into feathers of light,
rising, stretching, massaged
by murmurs
of a wind I can't feel, stirring
into an explosion of flight,
leaving my bewildered eyes
with only the
ripple of her joy.

He's younger but he slides
just like her.
The class clown of '74,
letting the sundogs pull
his vintage '56 hiccup
through a tunnel of
spinning bottles
and trombone trees,

lands on a
capsized spotlight
where all jokes
have the same punchline.

He meets his father
sliding up the
fourth-grade slope,
his rope
is braided with
skinned knees,
first dates, baptisms
and secret
fishing holes; his
footsteps simulate
the wings of an
exuberant escort,
and the laugh is on
the knots
of time.

5-31-03 (for Mom & for Reid, my classmate
who died 5-23-03 at age 46)

(When I'm scared,
she hugs me with her wings.
When his family cries, will he
drop daffodils at their door,
ride a shooting star, or
hug them with a sunrise?)

Ode to Lisa
(My Shining Star)

Strangers and friends sweep
the edge of our days;
clutter our sight like the
blurred Milky Way.
Our souls are like clouds
trapped in a dry cell...
with no love breezing
through,
we don't travel well.
Smothered in darkness
like an Idaho noon,
horizons shrink inward and
dreams are entombed.

But songs will break
through;
sun kisses our soul
when we reach out to find
the lost half of our whole!
Many sizes, shapes, places,
our star friends will be
surprising us when we most
need to be free.
A light for our path,
a voice over the phone...
a ready reminder
we're never alone.
A laugh when we're silly,
a hug when we're blue...
a sounding-board bouncing
our brain-storms and views.

(I've not written a poem
since the year '86...
I've forgotten so many
verbosity tricks.)

This poem is for Lisa,
but words can't portray
the black hole that you fill
with your sunny display.
You're a short little squirt
standing tall in my heart...
your star shoots right over
what Montana will part.

I envy the stars and the
birds
who are free
to fly over the stuff
that traps you and me.

My sister, my friend,
my niece,
have no doubt:
our love is the essence
of what life's all about!
You carry me. I carry you...
Forgiveness is not what we
ask,
we just do.

So remember one thing
as I wrap-up this poem:
I'm there on your shoulder;
you're never alone.
Dancing days, singing heart,
my life's better by far
because I have Lisa,
my bright, shining star!

(1997)

233

White Feather

The last
golden
maple leaf
shivered
in a shrouding fog over the
pumpkin-hearted robin,
splashing his
last bath.
October's closing sunset
subdued
the clicking ruby slippers and
foolish wooden noses,
shooshing the mockingbird and
cloaking us in a silent cage,
concealed
in the closets of sandcastles
until our frogs are kissed.

A lonely white owl
swooped into the moon when
the vulnerable light
spiraled and
crashed like spilled champagne
on the rocks.
All sand dollars but one
were exchanged
for cold hard splash
as the last sailboat folded
behind a gray
dumpster
fringed with the droppings of
dead dreams and a
single,
shivering
white feather.   October 25, 2000

235

Wrapped In a Riddle
(The Lost Key)

She dropped to her knees for a Rubinstein hug
and found herself wrapping a riddle:
"Why can't we live where sun shines 'til it sets?"
he coughed his smooth canine submittal,
"How can my old bones contain my young heart;
can you unleash your sad, sensible mind?
Let's cross the wide valley, climb over the crown,
find the bridge that obliterates time
through orangutan mist, 'til your nose can't deny
the sweet dust from Pocahontas' new shoes…
then you'll find Groucho Marx for a laugh and a hug
and Ben Franklin will lend you his muse!"

So the first night they found, in the Mission Bell Woods,
a tree house where eagles would meet,
sharing words from the whispering womb of the trees
in a language that Rubinstein speaks.
They awoke from an evening in Mars' southern glow
where raccoons had been speaking in rhymes…
they stretched and the sun tried to swallow the scent
of the trailhead that Ghandi designed.
So they stepped off the roof, slid down an old pine,
and the kit foxes scattered from view,
leaving kangaroo rats with mouths full of seeds
in a blue field that forest once knew.
They searched through the blossoms and burrows for clues
to a stream breathing messed destinies
of the stumbling fools and bumbling schools
since his birth babbling with Hercules,
"What do you want, what do you want?"

moaned the chorus of specters within,
"Sip from our ancient tears for visions and fears
from Gomorrah to Goualogo thin.
You will witness the setting of Rameses' god Ra
and Odin's army of Valkyries brave…
you will pray that the Norns break the Ragnarok spell,
and wonder at mankind the slave
to the evolving gods who are weaker than trees,
who drown dolphins in oils of Hussein,
who make us swallow blood off the chinamen feet
from the dogs they have murdered for gain.
"Do you want to see, do you want to see?"
(and Rubinstein's fur stood on end)
"We think that we won't take sip of your mead
for the brew is a most livid blend…
"Our thirst is inclined toward a raindrop fine wine,
not to ruminate ravenous ruins.
We want falcons to fly us through old fantasies
over roots humming tunes with the moon;
or we'll hitchhike a ride with my young dad so dapper
in his jalopy to yesterday's dawn…
we'll walk hand-in-hand with old Torger and Sjur,
picking rocks and fresh pansies for Mom
who will find the lost key that enlightens the box
of the gems of the proud potluck queen,
and she'll polish and fuss and remove years of dust
from me and the sad opalines…"

"Can you take us there, can you take us there?"
(the stream heard but did not understand).
So she turned to trail Ruby who already knew
they must run from this sourful land
back to the bridge and through the wide valley,
wading through ponderous weeds,

RUBINSTEIN (RUBY)

seeing now for the first time what they'd never seen
as the kangaroo rats dropped their seeds
to welcome the feet that retreated from view
now returning with humbler pace
to their haven carved out of zucchini and hemp
where the rhyming raccoon hides his face.

August 2001

Lolita

As the cool, creamy head
> *of my pint of brew settles,*
Lolita plays tunes with my
> *hickory cello*
on a circular stage, wearing
> *red velveteen...*
she makes "Danny Boy" sound
> *just a little obscene.*
I stand to applaud, but
> *just as I do...*
my wife wakes me up with
> *a cup of brown blues...*

April 2001

(written for a contest to win an Irish pub...
needless to say, someone else won...)

PRISM SHOWERS

Eyes glow
in my imagination and I
am tethered
to a specter who whispers
distorted memories of
vintage regrets.
Rampaging shadows claw at
the walls of my pride but
are scattered by the waves
of Grandma Anna whose
ocean ride is still
the buoyant part of me.
Rising from the vortex of
snarling foam, golden bubbles
are amused as fireflies caged
in chicken wire.
The evanescent demon dance
drowns beneath
the ascending bouquet which
transcends the sun,
tossing prism showers to
the imprisoned.

8-16-00

AUNT HELEN TELLING BROTHER
HOWARD THE WAY IT IS . . .

Aunt Helen
March 22, 1997

Aunt Helen died just as the eternal winter was ending. She took a look around and decided this wasn't worth fighting for anymore. She didn't take her checkbook or her bingo markers or her cat or her car or her camera.

The bills keep coming in, her clocks and electric blankets and coffeepot and pellet stove still operate perfectly. Her hairbrush, calendars, bowling bag and shopping lists are waiting, frozen in the moment she last used them. The birds still splash in her birdbath, and old long-distance friends call to chat and salesmen call to sell. The potted flowers on her deck are blooming in the spirit of the new spring season. Hungry hummingbirds hover near her giant fuschia, and her cat sleeps on her bed.

Her life was full of special things and people which made her happy and comfortable. The walls reflect the voices and laughter of many friends, sharing jokes and stories of adventure. Marathon games of spades and scrabble lit-up the wee morning hours. People loved by Helen died in this house, and new generations visited.

Large pans of lasagna, over-stuffed pork-chops and more massive culinary feasts were served to small armies. Waffles woke us in the morning as the fog slowly drained from the valley below and sun dried the deck. The traffic hum of Laureles Grade gave subliminal rhythm to the day.

The walls are shrined in pictures of dogs who would not let her travel. Casper tried to live as long as her, but failed two years ago. Snoopy was Ed's tug-o-war champ, and his likeness resides in drawings and jewelry and ceramics and stitchery. If you listen closely when you pull into the driveway, you can

almost hear their barks of defense. Ed and Casper are resting under the oak tree in little boxes, waiting for Helen to catch-up to them so their journey will continue together. They will travel by sea, to a place where they won't need medicine or money or keys or a warm coat; no leashes or flea-baths or Pupperoni's. They are free. They've graduated to the place of white light and love. Their spirits can visit us as we trudge behind in our stodgy, petty chores, but we can't sit down and chat anymore; we can't hug or swap secrets and recipes. We won't share movies or walk to the mailbox or plant jades and roses. That's not Helen's job anymore. We had so much in common, but now she's gone some place where we can't follow. We have been left behind to continue our search for The Purpose…and hope that someday we will catch-up to her and continue the journey together.

I will miss the mischief and love and feisty spirit that flashed from her sky-blue eyes. I will miss Aunt Helen, because she was my friend.

LISA'S BIRDHOUSE

The Unflown Frontier

(Happy Slice of Air: version 1)

With eloquence and urgency
the gyro-dance elopes
and feathered strokes spell destiny
to aerobatic heirs of hope.

Pigeon twitters on the pine
persuade a threshold pirouette...
the baby almost feels the breeze that
whispers tales of old regrets.

He sees his own captivity and
the tragedy of doubt...
he seizes certain jeopardy
with one diminutive step out!

His tumble is a brave ballet,
then luminous ascent;
he inspires darker spirits
to unequivocally repent!

Somehow, he knows he won't come back...
So Much! So Far! He strains to see...
(Do colors taste? Do raindrops hurt?
Do butterflies teach bravery?)

(Are stars above for each brave quest?
Am I too late to leave my nest?)

The moment comes, it comes for all...
epiphanies for large and small!

Empty sky. Silent tree.
Breathless serendipity!

August 2000

TRAPPED

Thirteen screaming demons
smothered the twins
in a trap
of traditional rust,
slammed flat
and forced to eat
the poison
of foreign snakes, farmed
by wise men.

No horses of any color
came to their rescue,
and the days
wrinkled
into one hideous night.

Green ghosts
seeped through the keyholes
to soothe
homesick dreams of
their rosy Roosevelt skies and
wild horizon dancing
to the hum of crystal
cottonwoods.

Mummified
and surprised, they
despised the speed
of the new demon, tarring
their tiny patch of high blue
and cinching
the wretched wrap over their
last twitch of hope.

April 28, 2005

9:00 PM, Paradise

July 18, 2005

A man and his car died yesterday.
They launched a westbound flight
over my woodland paradise
and crashed
through the delicate trestle
of blue-tip pines.
Only the solemn shadow
of the old Gnarly Wood
could share the splintered prayers
of this unscheduled sacrifice.
Could he hear
the wailing nighthawk
over the spin of
twisted tires? Did he feel
the wind, brushing the
buckled grass
from his face?
When the sunset
wrinkled into a cradle
around his worries,
were his weary eyes
smiling
at the halo of sacred eagles,
revealing
the flight path
for his soul?

KEVIN & SONS WITH A GIANT

Time Grows By

Here is the home of my poem:
here is the tree who stands alone -
look how tall, in spite of all
the meteoric powers!

Please tell a story to this zygote of 40!
Your braided bark moans with lost moments!
Only you really know if a bored UFO
is the artist who visits the crops…
and who designed space? And did you see the race
of the chariots golden decline?

Did T.R.'s Rough Ride stop the wild genocide
of frenetic teeth eating your fate?
Did you nurture his styling; were you so beguiling
with the sunshine caressing your crown
while it simply refused to touch his shabby shoes
and so humbled, he promised a life
spending nickels and quarters protecting your borders;
saddled tall on his new savings plan.

Only you and the stars can explain all your scars
as we sift through the topsoil of time…

Do your roots hold the years of pachyderm tears;
were you angry or frightened by flames
started by ancient fools who bred all the tools
that skewer our skylines today?
You never hurry, but I think you must worry
over what's lost, long before it's been found.
Every good human notion betrayed by emotion,
every knot that's been sliced, not untied;
the tradewinds of dreamers snuffed out by schemers,
and postcards of love, lost at sea...

You've witnessed our race at spin cycle pace
slamming into the boundary of time;
our untangled control falls into a hole,
chunks of sunshine are splattered away
and it feels like hell where root-dwellers dwell...
...in crumpled comfort, I see your design:
my blueprint for home: happy, alone,
watching my tree, watching me.

12-05-01

(Letter to a Wounded Friend)

September 10, 2005

My beautiful friend,

It's been a year and a half since I hugged you. I thought I would only be away for a month, but these wretched feet do not heal; they betray me and will not take me to you.

I miss you! Now, I am told, there is a 6-foot wound twisting through your body. What is it? How can I help? My heart is yours; you must be strong and wait for me!

Heal yourself, and I will heal myself, and we can have a wonderful reunion. You will dance for me and sing in unspoken whispers. Our eagle will laugh and tickle your tall branches with his feathers. My spirit will be your child again, bouncing in your strength, and I will hold you until our breath becomes one and nothing else matters.

Please, don't lose hope! If you fall, my soul will shatter into infinite homeless pieces. Only you are my comfort, my courage, my vision, my pulse. You are a celebration! Yes, I hear the other trees, but it is only young chatter.

If you must leave, I must follow. I will stumble to you and plant my ankles with your roots so that we may die together.

I love you!

♥ ~ me

♎︎

TICKLING MY ROOTS

1886 : 1978

I.   Yes, I am from Norway!
My great-grandma
packed me into her
future, put me
in a strong wooden box,
snuggled in with
wrapped dishes,
pewter cups, and gold
pocket-watches,
floated me
across the ocean
on waterproof
dreams and
determinations.
When the
American shoreline
pulled us in, we
found our trail
under
the light of the
Big Dipper,
following it
to a bump in the road
at Beaver Creek.

Great G'ma, baby Thelma,sisters,mom Anna

Claiming a patch
of wild
Dakota prairie, we
planted our pride
in the benevolent
soil. We became
perennial
Americans.

II.   I am old.
I am
the centennial spirit
of a Telemark toddler
who slipped
through the fingers
of the fjords
and turned boldly
to meet the
bright new land.
I am the love
of hands
and the work they
do. I delight
in the colorful
patterns of woven
tapestries, and
marvel at a rosemaler's

brush. I caress
the soft curves
of hand-carved wood,
and take pride
in the patient control of
hard labor.
I am Norwegian from
the core of my
Bestefar's heart…
I feel the land in me,
on me, around me.
The mountains
are a nourishing hug,
humbling
my small embrace.
The sky
is a mind,
writing new
poetry every night
with illuminated
blue ink
which will not flow
from my pen.
The rivers
are laughter…
light…liberated…
the fjords are a

strong heart,
sustaining a land
which will never thirst.
This land is wise,
and it is old. It is
a part of me.
I am old.

III.   I'm new; the
seeds
of my garden
stretch
in the perpetual
soil until
their hearts
are big enough
to marry
the midnight sun.
I am an accidental
ingredient
in the family recipe,
sifting comfortably
within the hug
of old flavors.
I am
a lingering melody
in the memory

The magic sands of Pismo Beach

of a gentle man,
curious cousins and
new friends.
I am here, I am
everywhere, like
a beach celebrating
the old sea; it
washes over
and into me,
tickling
and teasing me
with hints of a
dancing horizon.
Stumbling toward
the restless rhythm,
I abandon my
heavy feet.
Look, how easy it is!
A familiar old
Lillehammer laugh
bubbles up and
fills my weightlessness.
I am new!

Telemarksstabbur fra 1666.

Norway-Europe Journals of Adventure

These words are the heartbeat of a North Dakota farm girl, jumping over horizontal borders into a vertical world. The faces and places of 1976 & 1978 are jewels, shining brightly in the shadows of older years.

Saturday, May 15, 1976:
(7:00 a.m. Norway time; 1:00 a.m. back-home NoDak time)

The sun is shining warmly on Bogstad Campground here in Oslo, and it's hard to believe that I missed a whole night's sleep, because I'm _so_ wide-eyed! Yesterday (Friday) was quite a day. I got up at 5:00 a.m. in my little blue room on the farm. I managed to choke down half a Danish sweet roll, and didn't get uptight or emotional until 6:00 a.m., when I said goodbye to Mom. That was rough. The lump in my throat was bigger than both of us! Getting behind the steering wheel gave me something to do and calmed me down. I was due at the Winnipeg airport at noon and we were way ahead of schedule. Dad and I zoned into our own quiet corners of the car as Dan and LaVonne debated life issues with each other. With two hours to spare, we all agreed that the Winnipeg Zoo was the best diversion before my flight. I think my jitters affected my vision, because the faces of the zoo animals are only a vague blur in my mind!

At the airport, I didn't see anyone I knew from our tour group. We sat around while my nerves did somersaults in my stomach. Finally, Kathy walked in with her folks, George & Dorothy Lee, and I could almost breathe normally again. We got our baggage checked, went through the metal detector, and that was as far as our families could go with us. As they walked back out, LaVonne and Dan never looked back, but Dad hesitated at the door. I'm not sure if it was a look of worry or a look of wishing he could go with me, but he smiled and waved at me, and I tried to look brave when I waved back, but I was biting my tongue to keep from crying like a baby! I took some deep, calming breaths as we filed into the waiting room. Soon, the rest of our group checked in, including Char Rustan and Guttorm Brekke, our tour guides.

Finally, we boarded the plane - a Martinair Holland 707 - and we left the continent at 2:15. Lift-off was really exciting; like going up in an ever-rising ferris wheel; seeing the fields turn into little blocks, and the clouds became a cottony veil between us and the ground. We were served dinner right away and suddenly, I was more hungry than jittery; I wolfed it down! Kathy and I were seated a couple rows behind the wing - perfect view – next to a fun lady from Moorhead who'd been to Norway before; she had lots of helpful tips on where to go and what to do. We flew wa-a-ay up north, over the southern tip of Greenland with its ocean full of icebergs (huge white blotches on gray) and Kathy said the white ice spots on the ocean looked like grease spots on water.

We talked with some kids down the aisle until 8:00 p.m., when the stewardess told us to sit down for breakfast (what happened to supper!?). It was actually 2:00 a.m. Norsk time then.

Magical moment: we saw the sun set on one side of the airplane and rise on the other side within one hour's time. Too cool! We flew in over the northwest shore of Norway at 4:00 a.m. Norsk time. We stepped off the airplane at Gardermoen Airport and breathed our first Norwegian air; it was 1° Celsius (33°

Fahrenheit); exhilarating! We found our baggage and waited by the bus with Char, who would drive us into Oslo, just 44 kilometers (26 miles) south of the airport.

Norway has a <u>lot</u> of green trees, steep (vertical) slopes, beautiful modern homes, and narrow, narrow roads! Almost every home has a "stabbur" - a little square shack raised up from the ground by stilts to keep mice and other critters away from the food stored inside. Oslo is a very big city which we will see much more of in the next few days!

Our group totals 14 people; two older couples, one young couple, one single guy, five single girls, and Char and Guttorm. Except for the young couple (Sue & Bruce - from Canada), we are all from the Grand Forks, ND area. All of us single kids are UND students.

Char and Guttorm dropped all of us off at Bogstad Campground at 6:30 a.m. Norsk time. We're supposed to try to rest for awhile, but I don't think I can. It's really weird thinking that everyone back home is sound asleep in the dark, wee hours of the morning.

Two hours later: now we're sitting in the sun on the steps of our cabin, waiting and wondering...instead of sleeping, Kathy, Amy and I walked down along the lake across the highway from the campground. There are so many, many trees here, with the *hu-u-ugest* trunks sticking out of sides of cliffs! Dorothy would say, "ToTo, we're not in Kansas anymore!" We're hungry and curious about our first Norwegian meal. Most of us didn't bring Norsk money with us, and there may not be a place to exchange traveler's checks until Tuesday, because of the Syttende Mai national holiday on Monday the 17th.

A MOST SPECTACULAR TOUR GROUP
ON A MOST SPECTACULAR TOUR!

The Streets of Oslo

Goddaggen! Hva gjørte du i dag i Norge? Mye tinger, mye, mye tinger!

It's still Saturday, 8:00 p.m. Norway time now (I have been separated from the North American continent for 24 hours; I've been awake for 33 hours!).

This was a full day of piling in and out of our van throughout the inner city of Oslo. Thanks to Kathy and her elbow, my eyes were closed for only small parts of the tour. Suddenly, I'm soooo tired, and I couldn't handle the cradle-effect of the warm sun and swaying of the van.

Downtown Oslo has many cute shops - something for everyone (even poor students). Kathy and I made the big decision that she will collect spoons and I will collect patches to remember each place we visit. I'm not supposed to spend more than $50 a week while I'm here or I'll run out of money, so if I'm not careful, I'll be eating my patches!

We had our first meal at an outdoor sidewalk Norwegian restaurant; was that menu confusing or what! I ended up with something I recognized (fish'n chips), contrary to some other puzzled folks who had to take a mystery tour around their plates. When you're hungry, it's all good, even if you can't identify it!

While wandering around, taking pictures, I had my first contact with the native male species...he was one very drunk Viking, and I don't know what he said except something like, "You're my friend, aren't you...where you from...what is your name?" as he stumbled around me, close to my face. I just said, "Jeg forstå ikke, jeg snakke ikke Norsk...and I've gotta go meet my friend now, Bye!". Nice first impression, there!

My first people-watching note is that women wear hats here and more men have tattoos than back home!

We all met at the van at 5:00 and drove up to see the tallest ski jump in the world, the Holmenkollbakken. There's a great view of Oslo from the top, but you could never pay me to jump from there! G-g-gulp. We visited a ski museum which included a 2500 year-old ski, used in early polar expeditions. We stopped for coffee at the ski jump cafeteria and everybody was so burned-out, we unanimously agreed to go straight to our campground and <u>finally</u> catch some z-z-z-z's! Tomorrow's going to be a big day: to Vigeland Park and Bygdøy!

This momentous 48-hour day is ending, but not before totally messing-up the timeclock in my head. Uffda! Now, the sun has just gone down and brrrr, it is instantly cold. What will be more painful, a shower now or in the morning? I don't want to catch pneumonia this early in the tour...

Sunday, May 16, 1976:

We got up at 7:00 this morning and hit the road by 8:00 and haven't been back since (it's almost 7:00 p.m. now as I write). We saw a lot of stuff today, but still haven't hit Frognerparken with the Vigeland sculptures...of course, it's still light out, and I'm writing this while sitting in the van somewhere uptown, waiting for the group to round-up. I really like just riding around these crazy, skinny, fast-paced, curvy, criss-crossing, confusing streets of the city! Today I didn't have the problem of dozing-off all the time, because I got a good night's sleep last night!

Fountain square, downtown Oslo

We started the day with a smorgasbord breakfast at the Hotell Viking, for 18 kroner ($3.00). It was a feast: corn flakes, poached eggs, crunchy rye crisp, bacon, geitøst (goat cheese), lots of breads and strawberry jam, and more! After breakfast, we went to Sunday services at an American Lutheran Church with beautiful stained glass windows. We had coffee in the basement of the church and watched the Norskie locals mingle with each other. If you were filming this and turned the sound off, it would look like any church basement in AnyTown, USA. Surprisingly, nobody in the group came over and talked to us.

We moved on to the Folkemuseum and found ourselves in a 16th century village with sod-roof houses and all. Those early Norwegians were <u>short</u> people! The doors would knock my head off if I didn't bend down, and the beds were no longer than my arm span! Kathy would be of above-average height if she lived back then (she's 5'2")! One guy told us the beds were short because the Vikings slept sitting up, with their armor on, always ready to fight...but if that were so, wouldn't there be longer beds somewhere for the normal folks who weren't Viking warriors? Also, I saw my first Stave Kirke which is pretty amazing, even to someone like me who's never built anything out of wood.

From the Folkemuseum, we moved on to the humungous Viking ships in Bygdøy. These ships had been buried over 900 years, under huge dirt mounds with the owner and all his possessions. Everything, from beds to tools to carts, was included to prepare him for the afterlife. On the water, it took 30 men to row one of these ships. Next, we saw the KonTiki raft, on which Heyerdahl drifted across the Pacific Ocean, from Peru to Polynesia. Finally, we walked through the BIG ship "Fram," from Nansen's polar expedition, 1893-96. It was HUGE; it was equipped with everything, even a dentist, a piano...everything! The "Fram" was also used by Roald Amundsen in 1910 on his expedition to the South Pole.

Next stop: Edvard Munch Museum, which also had some pieces by Vincent van Gogh. Only two pieces made me stop and ponder: "The Shriek," and van Gogh's self portrait. These were not happy paintings.

Down the street, folks were gearing-up for the holiday. We found excited fiddlers and high-stepping dancers, clogging in wooden shoes. We watched their energetic performance until it exhausted us and we headed back to our beds by 11:00 p.m.

Celebrating our independence

Monday, May 17, 1976:

Today is the Syttende Mai: on this day in 1814, Norway became an independent kingdom (with Sweden) after 400 years of being ruled by Denmark. Later, in 1905, Norway and Sweden broke up, too. Right now, I'm on the street (Karl Johan gate) that leads up to the Palace; I'm sitting on the steps under a big statue of some guy on a horse. We have been watching the big parade for a couple hours. There were many, many schools of marching bands and beautiful costumes. Many women were dressed in the traditional folk costume which represented their area of Norway. Kerry Hefta (from our group) and I walked around together and found ladies representing our "roots". I hope my pictures turn out ok, of the ladies from Telemarken and Gudbransdalen! I also took a picture of a cute little blonde girl in the children's parade. She reminded me of myself, many years ago, wearing a little girl's Norwegian costume for a special celebration at Beaver Creek church, back home.

YOUNG SHERIE IN TRADITIONAL DRESS
FOR BEAVER CREEK PAGEANT - 1963

TRADITIONAL GUDBRANSDALEN DRESSES

SYTTENDE MAI

WELCOME TO FROGNER PARK

KATHY & SHERIE FOUND THEIR
MEN IN THE VIGELAND STATUES!

After the parade, we all went to Akershus Castle, the Resistance museum, with artifacts from World War II, when Germany invaded Norway. Many displays showed torture techniques (water dripped on head, leg twister) and diaries of captured prisoners which were smuggled out in hollowed-out bread cutters, and pictures and little miniature scenes of the war-torn areas. It was both interesting and disturbing, to see what some horrible human beings can do to innocent people. We wandered through the castle grounds, finally sitting down on the high part of the lawn to rest our feet and watch some Renaissance dancers perform in beautiful costumes.

Finally, at 6:00 p.m., we visited Frogner Park. I'd been looking forward to this all day! The Vigeland sculptures are <u>fantastic</u>! I can't believe all this came out of one man! Fascinating: human forms from all phases of life (baby, kid, teen, young parent, old age), shown in all experiences that you can imagine, from anger, love, discovery of self, playfulness, pride, sharing, crying, worrying, loneliness, etc. The park around the sculptures was beautiful, too; so green!

We returned to our campground and had our own little celebration of Syttende Mai, with special cake and "Solo" pop (like orange crush, yum)! We just sat around and talked and told jokes and did tricks with forks...I think it's gonna be a fun tour! I really like the people in our group; the older guys of the two couples are <u>so</u> funny - especially Duane Hilden. Eric, the lonely single guy, has been very nice to me by helping me when we first got here and I couldn't un-do the knot that brother-in-law Dan put on my backpack, and then the whole backpack fell apart when I tried to put it on. *Ta-da.* and now for my *next* klutzy performance...! After our little party, Kathy, Kerry, and I tried to call our Oslo relatives again, but none of us had luck. My phone stole a kroner from me! Well, my right ear is plugged and my face is burned from the warm Norwegian sun, but I'm happy, and it's 10:40 and I better hit the hay.

Elverum shenanigans

Tuesday, May 18, 1976:

The day started with all of us sitting in the sun on the front steps of the Rådhus (Oslo's Town Hall), waiting for Guttorm and the van. We traveled north, and I am now writing this in a nice, cozy cabin by Elverum, where I can hear the rushing water of the Glomma River behind me...this place is just *the most* heavenly, beautiful, romantic place I've seen yet - AND it's where my grandmother Kleven (Dad's mom) came from - the Osterdalen Valley!! Elverum is Guttorm's hometown, and you can tell he's proud of it. It's a town of 10,000 but doesn't seem that big. Guttorm gave us a short tour of the museum, where outside they had old log cabins, boat houses, rafts, etc, from the old Osterdalen Valley. The trees, thick green grass, peaceful pathways and rush of thundering water were powerful and enchanting! Kerry and I wandered, daydreamed, and agreed we could happily relinquish our bachelorette ways for any prince with a home in paradise. There are no words to describe the *feeling* of walking through a dream forest of ancient log cabins and being hugged by the spirit of the woods. The rushing rapids are an unbelievable, awesome force. Guttorm said he once rode a canoe over that white water, and he was never so scared in his life!

Driving north to Elverum, we passed through many little villages and more gorgeous country. I wish my dad could have seen the farmer in a field, steering a horse-drawn plow. We were driving too fast for me to get a picture of it; Kathy says Guttorm would have stopped if I'd asked him; I guess I need to learn to "speak up" for myself. Oh well. We also visited the Eidsvold museum, which is a "mansionous" house where the Norwegian constitution was signed in 1814.

Our first grocery-shopping experience almost got me kicked off the van! I bought some øst (cheese) and brød (bread) for Kathy, Kerry and I to share on the road...and the cheese <u>stinks</u> worse than a never-cleaned out-house. Phew! We hid it under the seat in the van, and still people can smell it! Bye-bye cheese, hello yummy yogurt and raisins!

The night of May 18th was like something out of a scary movie. It was around 11:00 and pretty dark and quiet. I came back alone from the showers. I was alone in the cabin, so I settled down to write on a post card until the rest of the girls got back from the showers. I heard footsteps outside the cabin door, but the door didn't open. Suddenly, I heard someone climb on the roof and scuffle and stomp back and forth, and then someone else was scraping something against the walls. I was just petrified...and very <u>stupid</u>, because I should have jumped to lock the door, but instead I just stayed real quiet, and finally I heard them jump off the roof and disappear. Soon after, the other girls came back, and when I told them about it, they poo-pooed it all like I was making it up! But then the noises returned, only worse! We didn't scream or run, but man, were we shaking. They knocked down the bottle holding the window above me, sticking their hands through the window and breathing heavy, and then they ran to try the door, but we all ran to hold the doorknob, and we couldn't get the lock to work! All four of us were trying to hold that little doorknob (the door opened to the outside so there was no way to block it on the inside). Amy and I ran back to the windows every time the attackers stuck their hands through; we tried to hit their hands with anything we could grab! Finally, the climax was when Amy took the knife for our cheese, and held it over the window, ready to stab the next hand that came through, when to both our relief and anger, a vaguely familiar voice from outside the window yells, "Hey guys, it's just us, it's just a joke!" and we didn't know how to react. Sure enough, there was Eric, Sue, Bruce, and the other Kerry from our tour group, doubled-over, laughing. Kathy grabbed the knife and ran out to them, yelling, "That *wasn't* funny, you guys, that *wasn't* funny!" and they stopped laughing then, because Kathy looked like she wanted to kill them! So, we spent the rest of the night talking about our different reactions and how we would handle something like that for real. Amy was the most practical one of all, even though she said that was the most scared she had ever been. Kathy was the angriest, and our Kerry was the most nervous. She couldn't settle down at all; she just kept pacing. Me, I finally fell asleep from nervous exhaustion! I'm sure we'll all be able to laugh about this crazy night, but we will be smarter, too. We will sleep with our money on us, and maybe we'll each buy a knife or something, so we're ready for the rougher towns in Europe.

Wednesday, May 19, 1976:

I learned a new word today: "taxidermy". First thing this morning, we visited the Elverum museum, which was really interesting…at one section, Duane was laughing at me because I said, "these are the most realistic stuffed animals I have ever seen!", and they were real wolves, bear, moose, and other wild animals who had been killed and preserved to look like they were still alive. They don't do that to dead animals where I come from! This museum was full of old farm machinery and tools, pictures of old logging camps, lots of cool stuff. Kerry and I walked around in the peaceful isolation of the evergreens and found a nice spot to rest and eat our oranges and talk. She's still a little freaked out from last night. What can I say!?!

We left Elverum at noon and drove north. We stopped at Hamar (Fargo, ND sister-city), to see the ruins of an old Monastery which had burned at the Krig (war). Also, there was an old cabin which had been transplanted from Kindred, ND, as part of the sister-city thing. It had stairs connecting two levels, and it had been used as a church and a school; an American Bible was still on the stand.

We left Hamar and hit the road to Lillehammer. Everyone was in a real goofy mood, especially Guttorm, who was mocking us when we oohed and aahed over pretty things in the shop windows in Lillehammer. We came upon a neat outdoor dance and bar area, with a stage down at the base of a bowl-shape area, and tables at different levels all around it. The band playing was kind of mellow, not bad. The drinks were very expensive (pop was 6 kroner, or $1.10 and beer was 11.5 kroner). In Norway, you must be 20 years old to drink hard stuff and vote, and 18 to drink beer.

We're staying in a youth hostel (The Bellevue), which is really a beautiful white mansion, and all the girls, including Char, are together in one big room with bunk beds. When we got back from our showers tonight, a few friendly Norwegian guys came over to talk and welcome us to Lillehammer, I guess. They were pretty nice, and probably enjoyed seeing all of us in our wet heads and robes!

Thursday, May 20, 1976:

Bjørnstjerne Bjørnson's home was our first stop today, on his farm which he named Aulestad, north of Lillehammer. He was a famous author who owned quite the _most_ beautiful house I've ever seen! They say he didn't have much money, but I think they must be kidding. Gosh, the furniture, the tapestry, the bust statues and paintings were just gorgeous, and all arranged exactly as it was when he died in 1910. The dining room was glittered with silver pieces in a glass cupboard which had been built to hug a wide window. It was so sunny and beautiful! They had a room beside the kitchen called the "Pig's Stye," because it was the smoking room, which was the only room where people were allowed to speak freely. Otherwise, it was a closed-mouth, formally strict deal. This room had cute paintings of kittens around the hearth, painted directly on the stones. Bjørnson didn't allow anyone in his study except his wife. I love the bedrooms, with their cozy canopy beds. It looks like it would have been so much fun to go to sleep there!

We left Aulestad around noon and drove back to Lillehammer to visit the Maihaugen museum, which had a Stave Kirke where Guttorm's parents were married. Also there were farms set up to look like the farms of the 1400's and 1500's, when each farm had up to 30 buildings on it, and the buildings were set in a circle, facing each other. There was a special yard and building for each animal. For the daughter of the house, there were special quarters set up in a house above the rest of the buildings.

My feet were screaming at me, so I stumbled back to our room and put my friendly earth shoes back on, and then I joined the group for chow uptown. I ordered an 8 kroner meal but they misunderstood and gave me a 15 kroner meal, which was a feast: hamburger, potatoes, gravy, vegetables, uffda! Too much and too expensive for this poor student! We window-shopped later and I got more oranges for the road. I have $11.00 worth of kroners left and I want that to last me until Saturday so I can say that I only spent $50 on my first week here. Can I keep this up, nope, 'cause I have to get souvenirs, too!

16ᵗʰ century village

De Sandvigske Samlinger, Maihaugen.

Gaustatoppen —, Rjukan, Telemarks høyeste fjell — 1.883 m. o. h.

Touching my Telemark roots

Friday, May 21, 1976:

It's a long, curvy, beautiful road that takes you from Lillehammer to Bø, in the land of Telemark, where my mom's dad was born. It took most of the day to get there. Along the way, I noticed things that for sure tell us we're not in North Dakota anymore, like more picket fences, birch trees, baby buggies, and older people on bikes. I saw my first real mountains today; the closer we got to Bø, the more gargantuous they became, with snow at the top and vertical walls hugging both sides of our narrow, meandering road. That was exciting and I couldn't stop staring at the monstrosity of it all, wow.

When we pulled in to our dormitory home for the next 3 or 4 nights, Arne Brekke was waiting for us. He's not only my UND language instructor, but he is also my travel agent and my genealogy researcher. He gave me a letter from his friend, Mrs. Ragnhild Hagen, who had found some of my Lillehammer relatives! I hope I have time, later in the trip to go back and find them! Also, she found the Berge farm where my great-grandma Anne lived before she came to North Dakota in 1886. I had been worried that I would be on my own, hunting through the towns of Vinje and Rauland, to find traces of the old Berge family, but Arne Brekke said that they have changed the tour's plans, and the whole group will be going out to the old Berge farm tomorrow! I can't believe it! Things are working out <u>much</u> better than I ever hoped!

So, we all settled down for a hot-dog supper, when a lady walked in and asked for Sherie Kleven. I turned and met Ingebjørg Gravjord, who I think is my 3rd cousin. She and her husband Halvor have a house in Oslo and a little farm in Bø. My great-grandma Anne was sister to Ingebjørg's great-grandpa Olav

Midtgarden. Anne's son Ole had a daughter named Thelma who is my mom. Olav's son Halvor had a daughter named Åsne Åkre who is Ingebjørg's mom. Tricky stuff, but I think that's right!

Ingebjørg and Halvor offered to take me up to their farm, so I wolfed-down my hot-dogs and off we went, talking all the way! First, they took me almost to the top of the mountains; we walked around and breathed the cool, high-mountain air, and I took some great bird's-eye pictures of Bø. I picked up a couple pocket rocks for a souvenir. Then we drove down to their farm, a nice little setting beside a high, tree-coated mountain. They showed me an older building where Halvor's mother used to live. In the corner was a kiln-type stove, made out of stone with a little door that opens to the fire and a platform in front of the door to warm pots of food. Just like in the story-books!

Outside, their yard was full of blossoming pear, plum, and apple trees, raspberry and current bushes, potatoes, and an onion-type vegetable which I'd never heard of before (leeks??).

Inside their house, we had coffee, norsk cookies and lefse, and lost track of time. They are so nice and easy to talk with! Halvor loves language (so do I). He teaches English and German at a Gymnas (school) in Oslo. He told some funny lines about how Cockneys speak, pronouncing their "a's" as "oi" and dropping their "h's"...funny guy! He is very well-read; his favorite author is Agatha Christy. We talked about American movies, too; he liked "One Flew Over the Cuckoo's Nest."

Suddenly, I realized that I had the key to the room that I was sharing with Kathy and Kerry, and I knew I better get back to the group. I took a picture of Ingebjørg and Halvor and they drove me back to my room by 11:00 p.m. No one from the group was back yet from the dance in town, so I grabbed a shower and a few quiet moments to catch-up writing about this day! Tomorrow will be another biggie!

Cousin Ingebjørg & Halvor

Sveinung & Grandma's old clock/cupboard

Sveinung

Saturday, May 22, 1976:

Where do I begin to tell the story of this day?? It began with a fun "frøkost" around the table with the clowns, especially Duane. He's got a joke for everything, and even though he says the jokes are 40 years old, they're new to us and funny because of how he tells 'em!

Ingebjørg came by at 9:00 to join our trip to the old Berge farm. Soon, Arne Brekke pulled in with Mrs. Ragnhild Hagen, and it was time to go. I was "volunteered" to ride in the "ekte norsk" car, with Arne, Ragnhild, and Ingebjørg. Uffda! I had a general idea of what they were saying, but I needed Ingebjørg to translate most of it for me!

Guttorm's van and Char's car were following us, and we stopped at a couple old churches on the way and looked through the cemeteries. I didn't find any Kleven, Berge, or Midtgarden tombstones. We traveled into the Vinje area, higher and higher into the mountains, until we came close to the town of Åmot, which is where great-grandma Anne's farm was. Ingebjørg ran to a farm to ask directions to Sveinung Berge (he's the son of the man who bought the farm from my great-grandma). The driveway leading up to my "roots" was a very steep, narrow, grassy road. Halfway up, we had to park the car and walk the rest of the way. We were all panting for breath by the time we came in sight of the farm.

There were about seven buildings there, all old log-wood type except for the white, flat-board, 2-story house. An old, stooped-over man shuffled out the front door with a pail of water which he poured onto the ground as he looked up at our approach. We said our "God dag's" and I let Arne and Ragnhild explain "på norsk" what my relationship was to his farm! Sveinung B. isn't related to me, but by the time I left that old farm, I felt like we were related, emotionally! He had a long, sagging face with droopy eyes of a sad kind of color. He was so obviously touched by my interest in the old generation, and happy to show us around.

He led us into the half of the house which has remained unchanged since my great-grandma Anne and husband Halvor lived there (Halvor died before they came to America). Just inside the door, to my right, was an old wooden bed like I've seen in museums, but this one was special to me. It was short, about 5 feet long, with faded rosemalling and four bed-post pillars to the ceiling, webbing out above to form a wooden canopy. In the opposite corner was another bed just like it. In the corner to my left was a hearth-type fireplace, the one Anne used. It had a stone slab in front for pots of food. Anne's wooden table and chair were there, along with her grandfather clock and a cupboard with some of her old dishes! It all was exciting, but kind of sad, too.

Sveinung took us upstairs to find a table with farm documents dated as far back as 1772! I saw the Bill of Sale from Anne to Sveinung's father, with their signatures, and the sale price of 80,000 kroner. Arne kept saying, "oh du, oh du, oh du!" as we looked over those very old, limp, worn papers. The most emotional moment was when he led me to a wall and pointed to a picture in a frame. I couldn't believe it: there was my own house, back home in North Dakota!! My great-grandma must have mailed

This roomy residence was built by O. W. Berge , Sharon, N. Dak., who used our machinery. Concrete blocks are not only adapted for stores and dwellings, but they form an ideal and sanitary material for hen houses, horse barns, cow stables, pig pens, silos, granaries, troughs, tanks, well curbing, etc. The first cost is about the same as lumber, and as no painting or repairs are needed, the five-year cost is less.

Arne Brekke with a lucky horseshoe from
Great-Grandma's blacksmith shop!

that picture to show them what her new home looked like in America, and Sveinung's father liked it so much that he framed it, and no one ever took it down? Wow, I was speechless and in tears. What a moment!

I took pictures (I should have taken more but it was pretty dark in there), then we went outside. Sveinung showed us the blacksmith shop and two stabburs from Anne's time, and he gave me an old horseshoe which was hanging with lots of rusty old friends on a wall that looked like it hadn't been touched in a hundred years. Sveinung had a storage chest full of those wooden air-fans (bellows?) that you squeeze to build up fire in a hearth. He had made these himself, with beautiful carved designs. Arne bought one for 200 kroner, and I was sad that I was on such a tight budget that I couldn't afford one.

We remembered the rest of the group, waiting for us, so we said our goodbyes. When I said, "Takk for alt," to Sveinung, he shook and held my hand so hard and with such a great smile on his face that I knew I would never forget! Is it possible to form a bond in just an hour's time with someone who doesn't speak a word of my own language? Yes, I think it is, because my heart speaks his language.

Later, when we were all eating dinner, Ingebjørg said Sveinung told her that he wasn't physically well anymore and he had given the farm away to a friend, because he would be moving to a retirement home the end of this summer. That's really sad. What will happen to all that history, all those old things that tell so many stories?

Our group moved on to visit the home of a popular Telemark writer named Vinje. Mostly, he wrote poetry, and a young girl was there, singing his poems set to music. Her voice was mellow and easy; I wish I could have recorded her.

Look, Mom: rich relatives!

Late afternoon, Arne, Ingebjørg and I split away from the group and pointed ourselves toward Rauland and the Halvor Midtgarden farm on Totak Lake, where Great-grandma Anne Berge was born. We found it with no trouble, and introductions were made with the non-English-speaking Halvor Midtgarden family. Halvor was Anne's great, great nephew. He is the postmaster in Rauland. He has a twin brother named Ricard, but I didn't meet him.

The Midtgardens have preserved the old farm where Anne was born; they say it has been photographed and displayed in Norwegian heritage magazines, so it's quite popular! To get there, we climbed a steep, steep hill of pasture rising high above their modern house. Finally, we reached the house where Anne was born; it was built in the 1600's and stood, until 15 years ago, next to the lake, where their new house is now. The walls inside were decorated with beautiful rosemalling; there were old butter churns and awesome wood carvings on the old corner beds. There was all the old furniture that you would expect, along with the unexpected ceiling lamps!

What a *huge* contrast between Anne's two houses in Norway and the one she built when she settled in America! What a change of scenery, too! Here, there are snow-topped mountains on all sides, a huge, wide lake to the front, and steep, stony, rugged land which could only be used for pasture. There, in North Dakota's Red River Valley, there's wide-open rolling crop land as far as the eye can see!

The Midtgarden family is pretty well-to-do; I could tell when I walked inside their beautiful home. We sat down to a couple hours of constant Norwegian conversation, with very few translations for me. It was a little aggravating, being related to the person

This is my Great Grandma's bed!

beside me, and *wanting* to communicate, but not being able to because of the language barrier. Setting that frustration aside, I have to say I enjoyed the feast, which they called "coffee". There was "spekekjøtt" (dried mutton), "smørbrø" (sandwiches) with slices of fish from their own lake, donuts, cake, and "Brigg øl" which is a sweet beer, pretty tasty!

After leaving the Midtgarden farm, I nodded off to sleep while Arne and Ingebjørg chatted, and nodded awake again when we dropped Ingebjørg at her farm outside Bø. Hopefully, I'll see her again in Oslo, before I leave for home. It was midnight when Arne dropped me off and I crashed into my sleeping bag. What a day to remember!!

Sunday, May 23, 1976:

This was a pretty calm day, compared to yesterday. We all woke up late and then hit the road to Skien, where we wandered through Brekkeparken (a beautiful flower-filled place). I know Mom and her green thumb would have loved seeing this! Next, we toured Ibsen's adult and childhood home in the country. We got back to our rooms at 6:00 p.m., and I tried my luck with washing clothes in a machine that I didn't understand, but it seemed to do the trick. We all wound down with a cucumber and tomato supper while Char gave us a little Norwegian language lesson.

Before I forget, here are my two favorite Arne Brekke jokes so far:
"Have you heard of psycho-ceramics?"
"No."
"It's the study of crack-pots!"

-and-

"Did you hear about the queer spider?"
"No."
"He was playing with his friend's fly."

Monday, May 24, 1976:

We saw a beautifully rosemalled church today in Bø, and spent the rest of the day shopping. I got myself a silver ring with 3 little spangle links on it (which means I will have 3 kids). It was 61 kroner, or about $12.00. It turned my finger green. I wonder if I got ripped-off?

I'm not feeling so hot today; I have a scratchy throat and my stomach hurts. Also, Kathy and Kerry haven't been getting along so well. There is something about Kerry that simply bugs the heck out of Kathy. My normally very kind, tolerant, funny friend begins to grow horns and claws when Kerry's around. Kerry just shrugs and shakes it off, so maybe I need to stop being so super-sensitive. Sometimes, when their fur starts standing on end, I can joke and jostle them out of it and stop the cat fight. Not so lucky today! The three of us will spend the next $2\frac{1}{2}$ weeks traveling together through Europe and back, so I hope our individual pet peeves don't push us over the edge!

Tonight, we gave Char and Guttorm a surprise party for being such great tour guides! We had cake, ice cream, tea and coffee. We decorated the kitchen with printed toilet tissue, and made bows and signs for their chairs that said "Frøken of Honor," and "Herr of Honor." Guttorm's uncle (Arne Brekke's brother) came and played accordion and there was dancing in the halls and everywhere! Char and Guttorm are really good dancers. I'd like to learn!

Char & Guttorm

I don't want to forget this silly little song that Guttorm taught us. He's always having fun, mixing the English and Norwegian languages together. This song is to the tune of Bobby Goldsboro's "Oh Honey Come Back":

♪♫

"Oh Hilda come back, Jeg kan ikke forstå disse lonely kvelds er so forferdelig! Og den siste gang jeg så deg, seems like a hundred år siden. Back to disse arms that kan ikke vait, oh the joy of elsk, that used to smakt so morsomt, come back, to bare meg, jeg elsker deg, woa, woa, woa, woooaaoo.
(Speak this:) Oh Hilda, jeg vet jeg promised not to snakk about it igjen, 'cause now you belong to Knut. But if you ever need someone to love ya, and someday you just might, you know where you kan fin meg. Just call me, ship to shore, the number is (7777) sju tusen, sju hundred, og sytte sjue!"

♪♫

The heart of fjord country

Tuesday, May 25, 1976:

We are now much, much farther north, in the town of Flåm, surrounded on three sides by mountain walls, in the heart of fjord country! The mountains are high as the noon sun, and there's the background music of several small, medium, and large waterfalls speeding down from the high mountain snow spots.

We covered a lot of ground today, packing up and moving out of Bø by 8:30 a.m. We stopped in Eggedal for Kerry H. to check out her relatives while the rest of us meandered and saw another beautiful Stave Kirke. When we left Eggedal, we headed west, where the mountains aren't grassy anymore, but are more bare,

gray and rocky. Up and down, ears plugging and unplugging, we made it as high as the snow tops and it wasn't cold; amazing! The roads were very, very skinny and the cliffs down the side were soooo steep, and whenever we met someone, it was nip-n-tuck with the wheels and the edge of nowhere! We went through tunnels on the way back down; the first one was two miles long and real dark and foggy. That was my first tunnel, and as we entered it, Dummy Here made the wise question of the day: "How do you see where you're going?" The whole van said, "You turn your lights on!" Duh.

Finally, we stopped in Nesbyen for midday dinner. After chow, I wandered into a department store and was about to wander out when I saw a beautiful wall hanging, like a rug with a scene of a farmer pushing a plow pulled by two horses. The minute I saw it, I knew it was the perfect anniversary gift to bring home to Mom and Dad! It's not junky like what I'd almost resorted to (a shoehorn and chewing tobacco). It was 125 kroner, or $25. Now, the trick is carrying it the rest of the way, with my backpack. Guess I'll build some good muscles on this trip!

In Flåm, we met Guttorm's folks and walked around. It's a very little town but whoa, what a view! We were examining the little black snails by our cabin when the handsome, mustached guys in the cabin next door introduced themselves. Va-va-voom! One of them was from Helena, Montana. They hung around until Duane stopped in to talk. He said Melvin and Vy Anderson (the other older couple in our group) will probably be riding the train with Kathy, Kerry and me when the group breaks up on Saturday. This will be our first Eurail train ride; it's supposed to take us straight into Denmark. It will be nice to have familiar faces on the train!

Wednesday, May 26, 1976:

Today felt like two days, because the morning was spent in the bright, warm sunshine of the Flåm Valley, and the afternoon was in the different climate of cool air and white snow at the mountain tops over Flåm.

This morning, after a shower, we were invited to Guttorm's place for "coffee," which of course, consisted of a feast of food: waffles, raspberry syrup, blødkake with whipped cream, and so much more. It was set up outside, like a picnic, under the shady trees, next to a field of bright yellow dandelions.

To wear off those zillions of calories, we set out to climb up part of the mountain. I wore the wrong kind of shoes for steep slopes and my ankles were flopping every which way, so I had to go most of the way barefoot! I ran up ahead and turned around to take a picture of most of them, huffing and puffing their way up! They passed me up, and my bare feet and I went back down to watch them until they became little stick men, far away. I walked over to the hotel to cash a check and then sat on the dock as a *humungous* ship moved out of the fjord. A ferry moved up alongside and it looked like a little tug boat in comparison. As the ferry came in closer, it was pretty big itself, carrying cars and all, so just imagine how gargantuous the other ship was!

The hotel cafeteria menu serves chicken for 47 kroner, that's $9.50...Yikes! Chicken seems to be rare here. Come to think of it, I haven't seen one chicken anywhere since we arrived, only ducks. Hmmmm....

When everyone had rested-up from mountain climbing, we decided to go up the easy, scenic way, on the Flåm-Myrdal train. This was my first train ride ever; I loved it! It stopped often and moved slowly so we could see the view. Kjossfossen

FLÅM VALLEY

LESSON #1: DON'T CLIMB BIG MOUNTAIN AFTER VERY BIG LUNCH!

BREKKE FALLS

CRUISING THE FJORDS ON A FERRYBOAT

waterfall was musical, sparkling, wild, wet, loud, wow! We sat with Char, Guttorm, Duane & Kerry and it was a great trip. We came back to our cabins just as the sky opened up and it rained, and rained, and rained. We had a supper of bread, jam, and cream cheese, and the rain kept on coming. The fresh, clean Norsk mountain air smells sooo nice!

Thursday, May 27, 1976:

So, I came to Norway for many "firsts"; my first mountain, tunnel, waterfall, first airplane, train ride, and now today, my first ferryboat ride! We moved out of Flåm at 8:30 a.m., drove to Aurland and waited to board the ferry. A black cat came over and made friends with me while we waited, and I call that *good* luck, not bad! It was so exciting on the ferry! I loved standing at the front by the railing, watching the smooth progression down the fjord. Seagulls were flying above us; so beautiful with their wings spread under a background of cloud-high mountains!

The ferry stopped at Gudvangen, Guttorm drove our van back onto dry ground and we all hopped in and hit the road for the town of Voss. There, we had dinner where it almost felt like the States, because it was a pizza shop. Their pizzas aren't like the ones back home, though. I had a Hawaiian burger (num!) and we were entertained by American rock music playing on the juke-box! We window-shopped the streets of Voss, but nothing was open because it's a national holiday (Ascension Day).

We saw more waterfalls today than I could have ever imagined. We drove up a super steep mountain (Stalheim) and stopped at a spot overlooking a waterfall and the valley, deep, deeply below. Really neat! We could really smell the brakes heating up on the way back down from there.

We pulled into Ulvik around 4:30 and drove around for awhile. Now, I'm sitting on the top bunk in our cabin while the rest of the girls are out for a walk, burning off calories as I only exercise my right hand...hmmm, I should do something about this...

Ok, I dropped my pen and went for a tour of a dairy farm with Duane and Guttorm. I learned something new about cows. I had no idea that they can get sunburned when they go out after being inside a barn, especially if they have white fur. Is he pulling my leg?!? Duane milks about 75 cows on his farm back home and he had fun checking out everything. Me, I just saw a huge white room that looked way too clean for cows, and lots of shiny milk machines. If I was a cow, I'd rather be outside in a green pasture.

When we got back, we all settled in Char and Guttorm's cabin and sang songs and talked; a fun time; I'll miss this group!

Kerry Hefta is sleeping with rocks and twigs under her pillow because bad trolls sneak in and kidnap children who don't hide rocks and twigs! We'll see if we're all gone in the morning and she's still here!

Here's another song from Guttorm: ♫ "North Dakota, North Dakota, with the cattle and the wheat and the folks who can't be beat; oh say hello-ta North Dako-ta, and you just can't say goodby-yi-yi!" ♫

Friday, May 28, 1976:

This was the last day of our Norway tour group; now we're on our own for the next two weeks! I woke up with the same cold everyone else has been passing around. Drat. Still, it was

TROLLS

a nice day. We pulled out of Ulvik bright and early and pointed ourselves toward Bergen, stopping once in Øystese to stock up on groceries for the road.

Edvard Grieg's home town

It was noon when we arrived in Bergen; we split up in many meandering directions to investigate the city, the harbor, the old town area. We found the train station and made reservations for tomorrow's train to Oslo. Next stop: the Bergen P.O., where a letter from Mom was waiting for me! Bad news about cousin Merlyn Kleven, killed in a car accident. I didn't know him too well, but what hit me was that it could have been me, in my car wreck just one year ago! I would've missed all this! Gotta be thankful. Mom also hinted that Dad is nervous about driving in Winnipeg to pick me up when we land back home, so I will try to find a ride with someone else.

Starfish!! Colonies of starfish! They live in a pool of water (fed by the ocean?) near Edvard Grieg's home in Troldhaugen. Grieg was a famous composer and his home is on a peaceful hill with a shady back yard where he and his wife, Nina, are entombed. The tomb is halfway up the side of a vertical hill, with their names carved on a stone slab door. Grieg's house was gorgeous, with a baby grand piano and lots of wood, chandeliers and nature paintings.

We're in a campground on the edge of Bergen, and we just finished a yummy supper at Guttorm's cabin. It was fresh shrimp from Bergen's Fisketorvet (fish market), and we had to shell it ourselves, de-heading and de-tailing it. That's a new one for me, too. It was mmmmm good; really different and fresher than the breaded shrimp I've had back home!

It's a long road to the Little Mermaid

Saturday, May 29, 1976:

This morning at 8:15, Kerry, Melvin, Vy, Kathy and I said goodbye to the group, and Char drove us to the Bergen train station. We've been traveling on this train for 3 hours. It's noon now and we just stopped at the Myrdal Stasjonen (the same one our tour group saw on the train from Flåm, just a few days ago!). We still have 5 hours to ride before we reach Oslo. I'm catching up on post cards and a thank-you to Mrs. Ragnhild Hagen for finding my family. Kathy is trying to talk to a little Norsk boy who seems to be some kind of royalty? His mom says he is a son of a member of Parliament, and tomorrow there will be a new train that will have his name (Henrik), and his train will run between Bergen and Oslo.

We finally made it to Oslo! Now, we are killing time in the Hotel Viking until 10:50 p.m., when we catch our train to Copenhagen! We didn't want to wait at the train station because of the obnoxious drunks who wouldn't leave us alone; just trying to make friends, I guess, but really a nuisance! There are more drunks walking the streets in Norway because people here lose their driver's license forever if they're caught drinking and driving, no second chances.

Sunday, May 30, 1976:

It's 7:00 a.m., and it's been a tough night, trying to sleep on this train. The seats aren't very comfortable, and it's too hot in here. I woke up at 3:00 as we rolled through Gøtenburg, Sweden, and it was light outside and I couldn't fall back asleep. I had a strange dream about touring some old place with Char and being harassed by a couple guys who turned out to be pirates. They led us into a cave to their chief pirate who looked through our purses and when he didn't find any money, he started crying because he was a retired pirate and had no income, so we felt sorry for him and I gave him 21 kroner that was hidden in my shoe!

Now, our train is backing onto a ferry which will take us over the sea from Halsingborg, Sweden to Helsingør, Denmark. Then we will travel by land to Copenhagen.

It's 6:00 p.m. in Copenhagen; it's been a fun day! We shoved our backpacks in lockers this morning and hit the streets. The Wax Museum was our first stop; that was really something-else! I swear I was looking at the real people: Liza Minnelli, Louis Armstrong, Sammy Davis Jr., Danny Kaye, Raquel Welch, Alfred Hitchcock, Vincent Price, Richard Burton, Elizabeth Taylor, Snow White, 7 Dwarfs, Sleeping Beauty, Prince Charming, Nixon, Kissinger, Frankenstein, Dracula! Wow, they even looked like they were breathing! That museum will be one of the highlights of my visit!

The Tivoli Gardens is really like a fair, with wild rides, food and souvenir stands, pinball and gambling machines, etc. We didn't stay too long; we had to find the Little Mermaid statue at the edge of the sea. We walked, and walked...and walked! We passed by some houses where ladies (of the evening?) were sitting at open windows with prices posted on signs in front of them. Kathy and I aren't *that* naïve; we know what they were selling!

Finally, we could feel the cool winds from the Baltic Sea; we knew the Little Mermaid was close. We asked some local Danes, and they said it was just beyond the big fountain, ahead. Well, we were expecting something a little bit bigger than what we found; blink and you'd almost miss her! She's a pretty little mermaid, but she is awfully little. We took pictures and headed

The Little Mermaid

. . . and who is this? Is
it Odin and his team of
oxen? (enroute to Mermaid)

back the way we came, to meet our 9:10 p.m. train to Köln, Germany. Deutschland, here we come!!

Deutschland

Monday, May 31, 1976:

Kathy woke me in a panic at 3:00 a.m. because she thought our train was entering Köln ahead of schedule! With nose-prints on the windows, we looked for a sign and realized we were in Hamburg and still needed to cruise through Düsseldorf before reaching Köln. We were in a 1st class train car, and sleeping was much easier.

Back and forth, back and forth, over the Rhine River bridge! The city of Köln sits on both sides of the river, and we didn't have our act together enough to see everything on one side first, and then the other. After a long line at the Bahnhof information booth, we traipsed next door to the huge cathedral which could hold 20 Beaver Creek churches, I'm sure! Then, we did the Rhine River Shuffle to the other side and found a room at a Youth Hostel. Aaaaahhh, that was our first shower since Saturday morning.

It's a little confusing here, because Kerry and I have forgotten what we learned in high school German language classes, and none of us are familiar with German customs. Folks don't seem so friendly here or able to speak English. We found a MacDonald's restaurant and managed to order something familiar, and then we tried to visit a couple museums but they are closed on Mondays, bummer. We shopped a little, and I bought a pretty blue German beer stein and a doll in folk costume for Mom's friend Myrtle.

Kerry & Sherie - Köln Germany

We are sharing our room at the Youth Hostel with three girls who only speak German, and we used a lot of sign language when we first met, to try to make friends, but then we all gave up. English language is required in Norwegian schools, but guess what, ToTo, we're not in Norway anymore...

The three lost little American girls are going for a long, relaxing ride on the Rhine River tomorrow, before we grab the train to Vienna, Austria!

Cruisin' the Rhine

Tuesday, June 1, 1976:

Wow, $14\frac{1}{2}$ hours on the magical, mystical Rhine, and so many fun faces and conversations in our day; where do I start? We boarded the ship at 7:00 this morning and never had to pay a single Deutsche Mark (German coin) because our Eurail Pass covered it all! This excursion was cruise-n-view only; we weren't allowed to get off the ship anywhere along the way. This was such a treat for our feet, our backs, our nerves, and our pocketbooks!

So soothing, cruising along at maybe 20 mph, we started out in the comfortable, round-back, cushioned chairs by the big dining room window. We passed Bonn, and stopped at Bad Godesberg to pick up more passengers ("Bad" prefix on a town name means there are mineral springs & cures for rheumatism, digestive or kidney disorders).

On the banks of the river, we saw many monasteries, castles, fortresses and towers dating back to the 12th century! We heard tales of old sea-captains being lured to their death by songs of the siren mermaids. The Roman God of Wine lived in the castle at Bacharach ☺. We were sipping wine and feeling verrry relaxed. Most folks on-board were English-speaking; many were from Canada. We meandered around, to catch the views on both sides of the ship. We met a couple from Iowa; their son is a student at Ames University, where my cousin Curt graduated. As we poured our last drop of wine, we asked a guy at the next table if he would take a picture of the three of us, not knowing that it would lead into a very colorful conversation! His name was Julio, from San Salvador. He started out by asking us about things on our Rhine map, then he bought us a couple more bottles of wine, saying whoever got the last drop would be married soon, according to his custom. He was very cute and polite, but fun, and looked a lot older than he was. He was 19, and traveling with his mother, who had three more sons at home and she plans to take each of them on this cruise when they reach Julio's age. Their full names were Calle Los Castaños and Julio Rey Panama.

We moved out to the back deck after it stopped raining; the sky was so pretty with the setting sun lighting up the edge of the clouds, over the green trees and dark turquoise water...what a view! Julio was enjoying himself so much, he said he felt like running or screaming or something (what was in that wine?). We talked about clouds and old storybook tales of cloud-kingdoms, and Peter Pan; we talked about music and language. He taught us how to count to 10 in French and Spanish, and we gave him a little Norwegian lesson. Kathy told him that I loved to write, and he asked me to write him a letter some day. Romance on deck, right?? Ha, how I wish! I think his deep brown eyes were eyeing Kathy more than anyone. He collected all our addresses, and we parted ways when the cruise ended at Mainz. His mom kissed our cheeks goodbye, which was very sweet.

KERRY, KATHY, SHERIE ON
THE GOOD SHIP RHINE (!)

We had two hours to find our land legs and meet the train for Vienna, Austria at 11:45 p.m. Mainz is the home of Gutenberg University and Gutenberg Museum; I wish we had a little more time to see this! Gutenberg set up his printing press here in the 1400's. Also, there's a palace with an art gallery showing Roman and Germanic art. *Roman* art. Wow, so close, yet so far...

We came up on a guy backpacking aimlessly, too, who asked if he could walk with us to the Mainz station. He reminded me of cousin Roger Grimsley, with his sparkling eyes and quick smile, except this guy had a dark beard. He was from Canada, and we were laughing as he mimicked our funny American expressions, like why do we say "oh FOR sad, oh FOR neat, oh FOR dumb..." and why do we end our sentences with prepositions, like "do you want to go WITH?...". When we reached the station, he thanked us for our company, and boarded his train for Paris.

As we waited for our train, two American GI's came over. They were from San Francisco, now living in Germany. They live on base, so they don't miss the States at all...but then why are they hanging out at a train station, waiting for American girls to walk by?

Falling in love with Austria

Wednesday, June 2, 1976:

Here we are, in the very same country where Julie Andrews ran through the hills, singing the sounds of music! I really like what I've seen of Austria so far; the smooth, green hills and bushy trees (cottonwoods, elms, etc) are a refreshing change from evergreens, evergreens, evergreens. *Finally*, chickens!! We had to travel all the way to Austria to see our first chickens! They were cute and brown and didn't speak English (smile).

We spent 5½ very rushed hours in Vienna. Even though we had a map, we were like little mice in a maze, back-tracking. We saw a cathedral, an opera house, but the only thing I wanted pictures of was the statue of men-mermaids (mer-men?) and the pretty sidewalk café.

There were sparks flying between Kathy and Kerry today; Kathy thinks Kerry lags behind and Kerry thinks Kathy is too bossy. Me, I'm in the middle of it all. It will be okay again when we're not in such a rush.

We grabbed the 3:15 train; in three hours we were in Salzburg! The rain was pouring as we grabbed maps and a phone and tried to find a room. We lucked-out when we called the Elizabeth Pensionate, but the guy gave us screwy directions and we were mice again, in a very wet maze. My shoes were so wet, they squished! With the help of folks on the street, we found our home for the night. From the outside, it looks like a mansion where a rich family once lived. It's been turned into a boarding house. Our room is very, very nice; there's a big double-bed, and a smaller one in the corner which I grabbed. We have a sink, towels, a little dining table; there's pretty wallpaper and silky blue-green drapes and a big closet to hang clothes. We could happily stay here forever! It's only 80 schillings ($4.00) a night!

Tomorrow, we join the Sound of Music tour! I can't wait!

Thursday, June 3, 1976:

I am in love with Austria! I must come back someday and spend more time here. I could live here! Don't get me wrong, my native Norway is awesome and overwhelming. But the mountains here seem friendlier because they aren't so rugged; they are more gentle and spread-out. The countryside reminds me a little

Mer-Men!

of home, except the fields are smaller. Even the roads, the interstates and overpasses are like home! The only downfall is that it rains a lot, and their money is goofy – too many bills and coins for the tiniest purchase! 20 Schillings is only one dollar, so you have to carry waaayyyy too much paper money to make it last. Also, Hitler was born in this country, which is too bad. A beautiful land like this doesn't deserve to be linked to an ugly man like him.

We hopped on the tour bus at 8:30 this morning; the tour guide gave us lots of info about Austria: the country's population is 7 million; 5 million are spread about the country and the rest live in Vienna. Their unemployment rate is only 2%, and their crime rate is low. He said even though it's a socialist government, people are free to run their own businesses; for instance, he pointed out a bakery which has been run by one family since the 1400's! Austria is bi-lingual; kids start learning English in 3rd grade, radio disc jockeys throw in English words and phrases because it's "cool" and there are many English-speaking TV shows.

I got a close-up picture of a gorgeous swan in the lake where Julie Andrews once took a big splash, next to the Von Trapp mansion from the Sound of Music. We saw lots of scenes from the movie, like the brick wall where Julie sang "I've Got confidence," and in a nearby village, there was the "Promenade of the Trees" where Master Von Trapp got mad at his kids for sitting in the trees. Kathy and I got a picture of ourselves in front of the fountain where they sang "Do Re Mi."

The tour ended at 1:30, and we spent the rest of the afternoon in the old section of town. I got lost in the Mozart museum because I was so mesmerized by the miniatures of his opera-stage-settings, and I lost track of Kathy and Kerry. Later, they

Kathy & Sherie "Do Re Mi"

told me I missed the section where they displayed his first violin and pictures of his childhood. Drat!

As I write this, we are waiting for our 11:45 Zurich train. We met our first Swede of the trip; he just came over and chatted for awhile until his north-bound train took him away. So far, we've met folks from Australia, Spain, Sweden, Canada, San Salvador, Florida, California, Iowa, Michigan, South Carolina, Oklahoma, Texas, and Illinois!

Zurich to Paris in 48 hours

Friday, June 4, 1976:

How about breakfast on a park bench, next to a Bonsai dwarf tree? That's how our day in Zurich began, after a very uncomfortable night on the crowded train. We were crammed-in with an older Australian lady and a newlywed couple from California (Don & Dawn) who were going to Africa to meet his parents who are missionaries.

The Bonsai tree was outside the Botanical Gardens, which was free and overflowing with flora and fauna! Next, we mingled with the animal kingdom at the Zurich Zoo. We had some trouble with our tickets for the Tram (trolley), but a nice Swiss woman helped us; she was a teacher of Junior High students.

The Zoo was a refreshing change after so many museums, statues, and cathedrals! We made friends with seals, penguins, ring-tailed monkeys and pandas!

Kerry's had it with us; she's gone. Seriously, she wants to spend her last week with relatives in Copenhagen, so we helped her buy a watch and walked through the rain (the sunshine doesn't like southern Europe very much) to her train.

Our train to Geneva only gave us two hours to explore, before riding another train to Paris. Three people we met along the way all warned us about being careful in Paris because they don't like Americans so much and they won't want to help and they might try to take advantage. These three people were an older guy from Toronto, a younger guy from North Carolina, and a girl from Texas who's just coming back from there.

Lost in the Louvre

Saturday, June 5, 1976:

Whew, this was a frantic day in a strange land. "Wi-wi," yes, yes, we know we're on our own here; two Norwegian girls racing through the crowds of Parisians! I think they all pretend not to speak English; it's pretty hard to believe that all the folks we asked for help today could only "wi-wi."

Last night's ride on the train was the worst yet, impossible to sleep with all the other sardines crammed into the un-cushioned 2nd-class compartment. I wondered if morning would *ever* come. It didn't get much better when we stepped off the train; we just traded one discomfort for another!

The most confusing for us was the underground metro system (subway), with all those lines & numbers going every which way. One guy from Canada said he would help us; he spoke French fluently but very little English. Funny thing is, he left to make a "quick" phone call, and he never came back! There were no subway workers to ask, so we were just about to give up and go infiltrate the city on foot, when a guy came over, said he had been learning English for two months, and he tried to help. We understood him enough to figure it out, and we were very thankful (guardian angel?)! After we rode the subway a couple times, it wasn't so hard, after all.

The Eiffel Tower and the Louvre were the two things we definitely wanted to see. So many folks had told us we would be disappointed with the Eiffel Tower; I don't know why; the minute we set eyes on it, we thought it was fantastic! It's very big, very beautiful, and if my pictures don't turn out, I'll just croak! It only cost 13.50 Franks ($3.00) to ride the elevator to the top and look over the city, but we didn't have time because we had to see the Louvre, before our 2:00 train to Brussels.

We had our lunch (bread, jam, cheese and "Finley" orange soda), and rode the subway to the Louvre, where they wouldn't let us in with our back packs, and there were no lockers. Kathy offered to watch our packs while I ran in first, mostly to see the Mona Lisa and the Venus D'Milo. There wasn't time to meander over all the other things in there. Well, here we go, mouse-in-a-maze time again: the building was H-U-U-U-GE and I couldn't find an exit door anywhere near where I left Kathy! Nobody, not policemen, not ticket-takers, nobody could say anything but "wi-wi," so I just dived out of a door way on the wrong side and ran all the way around, very frustrated because (tick-tick-tick) Kathy wasn't going to have a chance to go in and see anything by the time I got to her. I swear that building was a mile long! Kathy was too cool and kept telling me not to feel so bad, as we rushed to the subway – we only had 10 minutes to catch our train! Uffda. We missed the train, but found another one for Brussels in 2 hours, which is the one we should have booked in the first place, if we'd known how much time the Louvre would take. We really screwed up our timing on this day!

Norwegian in Paris

Some "Joe Cool" black guys flirted with us and gave us some "Hollywood" gum which we didn't dare chew because they just didn't seem like trustworthy boy scouts; just a little tooo friendly, you know? We left the boys behind and hopped the train to Brussels (Bruxelles, as it's known here)! What a relief to let the train do the work for awhile. The northern France countryside was mostly flat, like eastern NoDak. We arrived in Brussels at 8:00 p.m. and after exchanging our money, we hiked up a long, steep hill to our Youth Hostel (is somebody putting rocks in my backpack?). Mom wanted me to call our neighbor boy, David Meldahl who lives here now, but only his wife Judy was in, so I just left a message. It would have been fun to see a face from Beaver Creek!

Our showers felt more wonderful than ever, and now we are spiffy again and ready for our last week in Europe! Wow, what a whirlwind!

Promenade on the beach

Sunday, June 6, 1976:

The morning train from Brussels to Den Haag, Holland took us through more flat land, with windmills, dikes, and Holstein cows. The sun shined on us all day and it was so much more fun than yesterday! It was a little after noon when we rode the trolley to Westbroe Park, known for beautiful roses which weren't blooming yet but it was still pretty. We took pictures and found a yellow-chandeliered tree with baby blue flower blossoms to shade us while we dined on crackers, jam, and cheese.

My friend "Walter" is here! He's the pigeon I met by the Little Mermaid in Copenhagen and he's faithfully followed me everywhere, for a bread-crumb delight in Salzburg's sidewalk café, to dinner at the Eiffel Tower, and now here. Can I take him home, please can I, can I?

Winged friend Walter & company

The Atlantic Ocean!!!! Wow!!! We walked from Westbroe Park to the beach "Promenade," which was a fair, with rides and games, just like the good old Fargo Fair, only much more special with the sandy beach and ocean waves! We walked out on the dock and breathed the salty air, wandered through the beach shops (I got a wooden shoe-boat, Kathy got a spoon and charm but lost the little package somewhere along the way...bummer).

On the trolley from the beach to the train station, we made friends with some German-speaking guys with brown complexions like from Puerto-Rico, maybe. Their English was pretty rusty, but their body language made us much more comfortable than the guys we met in France! They weren't going to pinch our butts like the dirty *old* men on the Paris subway!

It's 8:00 p.m. and we have a couple hours here in Amsterdam before we grab the train to Copenhagen. We're sticking real close to the station, because of everything we've heard about this city. Just walking down the block and back, we saw drug deals under the bridge and dizzy folks walking & talking real strangely...the sooner we get out of here, the better!

North to Oslo with Vira and Bru

Monday, June 7, 1976:

We rode through the night in a comfortable compartment with a guy from Denmark and two girls from Oak Lawn, Illinois; we pulled in to Copenhagen at 8:00 a.m. and had four hours to wander before our noon train to Oslo. First stop: a bakery, for big, flaky rolls and milk; yum! We stocked up on bread and cheese, and then we took a slow stroll through a museum...but y'know, a museum is a museum is a museum once you've seen as many as we have!

AUSTRIA

BELGIUM

HOLLAND

Our nine-hour train ride from Copenhagen to Oslo was fun, thanks to Vira and Bru Gustavson from Philadelphia. They've been married 40 years and still get a kick out of each other. They were both born in Sweden and have that American-Scandinavian accent that reminds me of home. They brought some friends into our compartment, and listening to them talk & laugh was just like listening to Uncle Mons and Clara and Mom and Dad talking around the dinner table! We were in the last car of the train, and I kept running to the back, looking for the perfect picture of a cow near the tracks. Bru kept asking me, "Did you get your cow?" I'm sure they thought I was a little weird!

Kathy's older cousin Ella met us when the train stopped in Oslo at 9:45 p.m. and we rode the trolley to her apartment. She is a good-hearted woman, probably in her 60's; a cozy grand-motherly type; she walks with a cane but it doesn't seem to slow her down. She set us up with a very cozy room and insisted on fixing "coffee," which, of course, was a hefty lunch!

Lillehammer wins my heart

Tuesday, June 8, 1976:

Today was my first contact with Kleven kinfolk in Norge! I left Kathy with Ella and took the 10:00 a.m. train from Oslo to Lillehammer. There was an obnoxious drunk on the car with us who kept spilling his beer and trying to wrestle with the kids across the aisle. I think we were all happy to get out of there when the train stopped in Lillehammer at 12:45! I found a phone and called a cousin named Alma Skaaden, who didn't understand my broken Norwegian too well. A man at the information booth called her again for me, and when she understood who I was, she welcomed me up to her house. I could have taken a bus, but I thought I could handle the 4-kilometer hike and save myself some money, silly me. It was all uphill, in the hottest part of the day, and I almost gave up! My visit with Alma was well worth the effort; she is a sweet lady with happy eyes and I felt a bond with her right off the bat. She speaks zero English, so it was time for me to stretch my Norwegian vocabulary! I would say, "Kan du snakke ikke so fort," and with a lot of sign language and scratching our heads and giggling, we patched it together amazingly well! My dad and Alma are first-cousins because Alma's mother was Ingeborg Kleven, sister to Even Kleven who was my dad's father.

Alma lives in a cozy, one-bedroom house, with old wooden floors and no fancy furniture, but very comfortable. Her old record player and her Bible are open and obviously used very often. She played some Norwegian Christmas songs for me, and we talked a little bit about God, enough for me to know that her heart is very sure that He exists and gives us hope for a heaven waiting for us! There are lots of fruit trees, berry bushes and flowers in her yard, and happy Norwegian birds. It's peaceful.

Many of Alma's sisters & brothers moved to Minnesota. Alma was the youngest, she is now 74; she never married. Her niece, Kari, who also speaks no English, came over to meet me and have lunch. I told them that I really wanted to see the old Kleven farm, so Alma called relatives north, in Vinstra, and I will be taking the 9:00 a.m. bus tomorrow to meet them. "Nei, jeg må begynnte å tro av den senga." I've learned more Norwegian today than all year in school!

ALMA SKAADEN & NIECE KARI

Wednesday, June 9, 1976:

It's 8:45 a.m. and I'm waiting outside the Lillehammer bus station for my 9:00 bus to Vinstra. It was hard to leave Alma this morning. She walked me to the bus stop and when it was time to say our "Ha Det's," she offered a handshake and I leaned over and kissed her cheek and we both had red eyes. In fact, I still have a lump in my throat. I feel like I've known Alma all my life, and I will never forget her smile, her young spirit and her patience with me, struggling to "snakke Norsk!" If I ever met someone who *glowed*, it was Alma.

Grandpa Even Kleven's mountain home

It's now 12:35, and I have an hour to kill...I'm in Vinstra, a small town where folks know each other. The town is at the bottom of a steep, grassy mountain, with a flat valley and farm land off to the other side. I found Olav Skaaden's house just where Alma said it would be, but he wasn't home, so I walked to the department store where he works. Olav only speaks Norwegian, but a nice customer stepped over and translated for us. Olav's daughter Hanne Lena will be home from school at 2:00, and then we will all go to the old Kleven farm together. Olav is Alma's cousin through her father, Simen Skaaden. I am related to Alma through her mother, Ingeborg Kleven Skaaden. So, this Olav in Vinstra is not related to me, but he's being a nice guy (for Alma?) by showing me around.

It's 7:40 p.m. now, and I am on the southbound bus from Vinstra to Lillehammer; my head is trying to absorb the whole day; I don't want to forget anything! As planned, I met Hanne Lena, who is 18 and speaks English very well, and she is very, very nice. She has long blond hair and a pretty face. Her mom died three years ago of a heart attack, so she lives alone with her dad in a 200-year-old house that is beautifully furnished. Olav gave me a hand-carved, rosemalled wooden spoon and plate, which he made; how nice! Hanne Lena and her dad really love each other, you can tell. She is worried about leaving him alone this fall when she goes to school in Yugoslavia. She's traveled quite a bit; seemed to like Italy most. We talked very easily, about everything, from split ends to alcoholics!

Also, I met a man named Pål Bakken, who turns out to be my dad's second cousin! His grandma Annie Kleven was sister to my dad's father Even. Annie's daughter Bertha was my dad's first cousin, and Bertha's son Pål is my dad's second cousin. Cool!

Pål, Hanne Lena, and I squeezed into Pål's white Volkswagen Bug and headed up, up, up the steep mountain side. We parked and walked the rest of the way up to the old Kleven farm ("setra"). All that's left are old stone foundations of the barn, two houses, the animal shelter, and the wooden handle of an old plow, and a square hole in the ground which used to be their cellar. The view of the farm land in the valley below was incredible! We were up so high, the fields looked like patchwork. Pål said he was the same age as some of grandpa Even's younger sisters and brothers; he visited them at the "setra" every summer, with all their cows and sheep feeding off the high mountain grass (it made their cheese and milk taste better). He remembers the kids walking to and from school, all the way up and down that mountain.

Pål had packed a picnic lunch, so the foundation stones became our table and chairs. Sandwiches, cookies, and pop taste exceptionally good in the high mountain air! Pål remembers the last person to live here was Even's youngest sister Thina, who wasn't married but had a baby girl named Anna. Anna died, and Thina moved off the "setra" and sadly, it's been empty ever since.

HANNE-LENA & PÅL ~ PICNIC ON
THE OLD KLEVEN SETER

Even's sis Tina at Kleven mtn. seter

YOUNG GRANDPA EVEN KLEVEN

Even was 25 years old when his girlfriend's family rode the boat to America in 1880. Her name was Anne Tronsdatter Anderson, she stayed back in Norway while her mother and brother settled in Starbuck, MN. Even followed them, settling in Webster, SD, and Anne followed him in 1885. They were married in America.

After I took pictures, we made our way back down to Vinstra. We bought some soft ice cream and cruised around until 7:00 p.m. when I caught my bus to Lillehammer.

Later...I was rescued tonight by two Mormons named Bjørn and Aksel. It was 9:00 p.m. when my bus dropped me off in Lillehammer, and both the bus and train station were locked up tight. I found a phone booth and was about to call some Youth Hostels when two guys walked over and in an American accent, asked if I was American and did I need help? They are Mormon missionaries from Seattle and Wyoming, living in Norway for two years "on mission" which is a Mormon coming-of-age thing, expected of young adults. They're supposed to "spread the word" of Mormon faith.

They walked with me up the Lillehammer hill to a very nice pension, just a half block from the Bellevue, where our tour group stayed a couple weeks ago. When Bjørn and Aksel said goodbye, they asked me to mention them to my Mormon cousin Gary, and I'm supposed to have Gary spend an hour with me, sharing his religion! Little do they know, Gary spent hours in our farm house, debating with Mom, when he first converted from Presbyterian to Mormon!

I have a room all to my own; just gorgeously comfortable, with my own sink, a soft bed, and freedom to talk and sing to myself as much as I want!! I'm happy!

Thursday, June 10, 1976:

After a good night's sleep in that soft, warm bed, I woke refreshed and ready to face my last day in Norway. I left the pension at 9:00 and pointed my billfold in the direction of uptown. I found a terrific store which answered all questions of what gifts to bring home for sister Gloria and family: a Scandinavian Fairy Tales book! In another store, for sister LaVonne and family, I got hand-carved wooden nut crackers (with Troll faces) and a little cup & saucer that says "Flink Gutt" (clever boy) for nephew David. For Kathy, I got the silver pin she wanted, and for me, a book all about Gudbransdalen.

I didn't go over my budget too much; I spent about $75.00 each week. I'm kind of excited about going home but I'm sad that this incredible trip has to end and only become a memory.

I called Ingebjørg when my Lillehammer train dropped me in Oslo; she rode the subway down to meet me at 4:00 in the afternoon. Good-Riddance to that crazy train station with all the strange drunks wandering around! We rode the subway up to Ingebjørg and Halvor's 4th-floor apartment, and the hours flew by! They got a kick out me because I am speaking more Norwegian now than when we first met. Ingebjørg showed me the family tree which she started working on after our day on the Sveinung Berge farm. She discovered that great-grandma Anne and husband Halvor were first cousins...oops!

Halvor translated a German fairy tale about the Pied Piper and the rats, while Ingebjørg fixed a meal of hamburgers with flatbread. Ingebjørg laughs so easily, and I feel so relaxed in their company!

It was 1:00 a.m. when we finally went to sleep, and four hours later, Ingebjørg was waking me, saying, "Wake up, my Sherie, today you get to go home!" After a quick bread & sausage & geitøst breakfast, we took the bus for Braathen's Safe, by the Rådhus, where the old tour group came back together for our last ride, to Gardermoen Airport. I couldn't find the right words to thank Ingebjørg when we said goodbye; "Tusen takk for alt," and " vi må skrive," just didn't seem to cover it all. Still, my most emotional goodbye of the trip was with Alma Skaaden in Lillehammer.

The bus to Gardermoen was packed to the brim with everyone and their souvenirs; it was fun catching-up with each other's adventures! We changed our kroner into American dollars, boarded the plane (Pacific Western Boeing 707), and at 10:00 a.m., Norway disappeared under the clouds.

Greenland

Hallo! It's 2:50 p.m. (Norsk time) and we have been stopped in Greenland to refuel. They let us all pile out and take pictures. This land is *really* barren. As we came in over the eastern coast, we first saw the cold, jagged, gray mountains poking up through snow caps, then solid snow fields for miles & miles, and finally the mud fields where we landed. It feels like no-man's land! The cutest thing to take a picture of is a mileage pole with multiple signs, posting the distance from here to various corners of the globe. We're supposed to board the plane in a half hour, to land in Winnipeg at 7:10 p.m. Norsk time, or 1:10 American afternoon time.

Later...I'm home!! We survived the smooth landing in Winnipeg, slipped through customs inspection, and it was a hot, humid ride

LIFE IS GOOD! (Sharie, Kathy, Kerry)

Triblet

to meet Mom & Dad in Grafton. From there, we drove Kathy to the HiWay Host Restaurant in Grand Forks, where her parents were waiting.

There was sooo much to talk about; I was just bubbling over! Pulling in to our farm yard was a happy time; everything is greener than I remember, and my Triblet kittykat will not leave my side (she missed me?), and there's a refrigerator full of my favorite food (mom's macaroni salad, yum); I'm 5-pounds lighter, and I'm home, home, <u>home</u>!!

(Fast-forward two years: it's May, 1978. In February, my dad died on a normal day, bringing in the mail. In April, my favorite uncle Mons died, also on a normal, active day at home on his farm. Now, most of my friends are graduating from UND and moving away to new lives somewhere else. I will be graduating a semester late, in December, because I couldn't concentrate on classes when the bottom fell out of my safe little world. Without Dad and Mons, I'm feeling more than a little lost. I took for granted that they would forever be sharing my life with me. This is a hard lesson on how fast life can be snuffed-out. I am about to learn that angels come in all shapes and sizes, beginning with one random phone call which leads to a Norwegian miracle for my broken heart...)

Monday, May 15, 1978:

Wow, wow, <u>wow</u>, DJ, here I am, riding to Winnipeg with Sam & Pete Johnson and my pal Mari; we just passed Canadian Customs, and I am just a couple hours away from boarding my midnight plane to REISE TIL NORGE!! We're hoping the check-in people don't notice that I am actually Mari's replacement.

This is the most impulsive decision I've ever made! Three days ago, Norway was furthest from my mind! Ron and I were hanging out in Scott's room on Friday night, watching him pack. Everyone's been packing and leaving; the quietness grows and grows....Anyway, Scott called Arne Brekke to confirm everything for Scott's trip to Norway in June. While they talked, I whispered, "say hi to Arne for me," and Arne asked to talk to me! He offered me a round-trip ticket to Norway for $250, taking Mari's place because she's going with Sam next month. Arne knows a farmer in Flåm who lets UND students stay with him, just for the experience of working the farm, and I would be welcome there!

When I put the phone down, Scott and Ron watched me go nuts as I tried to think it through and decide! We went to Burger King for one last dinner together (they left for their Fortuna & Larson homes on Saturday), then we parked ourselves at Wittenberg chapel and actually fell asleep there, talking so long and trying to savor each other's company to the last second!

I yin-yanged through most of Saturday: I'm going, I'm not going, going, not going...yikes! Good old rational Brad had almost convinced me not to go, but when I talked to Mari, she reminded me how much I loved my last trip and she thought this would be good for me. The clincher was when I called sister LaVonne on the farm. She's the last person I would expect to support this, but she blew me away when she got excited about it, too! Mom called me back and gave me the green light by giving me the money. I feel a little guilty about borrowing from her, but how can you beat this deal!? I bet the whole trip won't be more than $350 because I'll be working on a farm!

At Sunday morning services, Paul and I were ushers for a very dwindling crowd. After church, with only five left from our gang (Paul, Brad, Larry, Diane and me), we moseyed over to Happy Joe's Pizza. It was fun until the good-byes, especially with Paul. Brad's crusty humor came in handy for a change when he elbowed me and said if I ever run out of Norsk words, just say, "'Vil du på senga med meg?" That's the only Norwegian phrase he'll ever remember! I hugged them all and dived out of there before I made a crying fool of myself, then headed home to the farm to see Mom and get my traveling gear together.

Bright and early this (Monday) morning, Mom and I went to the bank together, and we had a little lunch before I had to leave her. I'm sad because she's still not her spunky self, and I can't do much to cheer her up. My weekends with her have been pretty quiet, but I think she likes it that way, having someone there but not being forced to talk. I know that she and Aunt Clara are kind of holding each other up in this strange new world without Dad and Uncle Mons. They have spent a lot of time together and are closer than ever.

On the road with Arne

Wednesday, May 17, 1978 (Syttende Mai):

It's 5:20 p.m. on this national holiday; I am writing this under a tree near an auto repair shop in Nesbyen while Arne finds what is wrong with his Audi rental car. Traveling with us is a family of three: mom Sue with kids Shelly & Matthew. When we reach Flåm, we'll all go our separate ways.

It's been cool and cloudy since we landed yesterday afternoon. The "magic" isn't here, not like my first visit in '76. Maybe it's the weather, maybe it's lack of starry-eyed companions, or maybe the tough year has worn me down. A small group of us rode the van from Gardermoen in to Oslo; the radio was playing the Eagles' "Hotel California" and one of the guys started singing along, changing the words to "Hotel Scandinavia," which stuck in my head forever! The van dropped us at that very hotel, and we walked around together for awhile; seeing Akershus Castle and window shopping. I split-off on my own and meandered aimlessly until round-up time for Arne's group at the Hotel Scandinavia. I was a little early and was flipping through postcards in the hotel lobby when a very drunk man weaved up to me, said he was from Greece and when he made sure that I wasn't married, he got right to the point that we should go up to his room and have a drink. He took off for the bathroom, saying he'd be right back, and I took off for the front door!

I saw a pay-phone line and decided to call cousin Ingebjørg and Halvor. The guy in line in front of me turned, speaking to me in Norwegian, then switched to English when he heard I was American. He is Rolando, from Columbia, South America, working on some kind of government job for three months. He seemed to be a nice guy, and we were having an interesting talk, so when the line had not moved, he suggested we go have a drink, I said yes. We had a couple Singapore Slings and shared philosophy of the world. When I said I needed to get back to my group, he said, "so you will abandon me?" and I said, "yup, sorry, but thanks!" He gave me his address and phone # and wants to see me whenever I come back to Oslo. He took my hand, kissed my cheek and then turned, hopped on a streetcar, and was gone, leaving me to wonder what was in the air, making these guys so friendly!?! VELKOMMEN TIL NORGE!!

This morning, after a short night in a small room across from Hotel Scandinavia, our little group watched the Syttende Mai celebrations until noonish, when we hit the road for Vestlandet! Hallo, hallo; the Oslo festivities weren't as exciting as they were two years ago, and I was ready to ride. Driving west with Arne has been more fun; he is singing and sharing silly jokes and local customs and history, etc.

A FELLOW NAMED INGE

"When Mary had a little lamb, the folks were quite surprised,
but when old MacDonald had a farm,
they couldn't believe their eyes!"
(an Arne original)

Thursday, May 18, 1978:

It's 1:00 p.m. and we're in Vassbygdi, 7 kilometers from Flåm. Since I last wrote to you, DJ, I've been exposed to mye Norsk kulture! We spent the night in a community of cabins in Østerbø, where we met so many nice people! I thought I was meeting Clark Gable when we first walked in to the dining area, but it was a fellow named Inge who made time fly with fun conversation (Men det var moro å prøve å snakke med han, og jeg synes han...got a kick out of it, too.). I was speaking better than I ever have (jeg skal snart ble flink å snakke Norsk!).

We took pictures, and finally went to sleep around 2:00 a.m., only to wake a few hours later to a warmer world; we drove through more tunnels and stopped in Vassbygdi å kjøpe frimerker og fikk mer penger på banken. There was an old church (Det var også en gamle kirke hvis vi så på); they were having a funeral there today. Also, Arne showed us his school, where he learned to speak German and English!

I am a Flåm farm girl now

We finally reached beautiful Flåm where we met Arne's brother and wife, Knute and Nellie; also Torstein and Kari Brekke. We dropped Sue and family into a cabin by the dandelion field, then

Arne and I drove up to meet Sjur Heimdal (reise opp til Heimdal gården og jeg møtet Sjur).

Sjur (pronounced shooer) is a bachelor, probably in his 40's, with thick hair behind a receding hairline; he has kind, expressive eyes and an oval smile. He's very nice and he can speak English. His house is a big, two-story with an upstairs porch next to my room. He is remodeling a new barn now, and he needs help with the sheep, the vegetable garden, and the housework. I think I will really like it here!

Friday, May 19, 1978:

It's only 4:30 p.m. and I am tired! We had a busy day on the farm! I couldn't sleep long last night because I had to rise early to help Sjur with the birth of a baby lamb. That was exciting to see! (Det er bare 16:30 og jeg er trett! Vi har det so travelt her på gården. Men jeg kunne ikke sov i hele natt, og vekke so tidlig å hjelpe arbeide i morn. Sjur har en sau som gi fødsel til en lamb denne morgen, og jeg så pa det! Veldige spennende!)

I walked to the grocery store to buy food for our noon meal. I cooked sausage, peas and potatoes; the sausage was a little burned, but Sjur ate it anyway (Og da jeg gikk ned til butikken å kjøpe mat for middag. Jeg kokt pølser og grønnsaker og poteter, og det var lit brenne, men Sjur spiste det i allfall!).

It's 11:00 p.m. now; tonight Sjur and I found something in common: music! He plays trumpet and violin and has a good ear for learning new music (Det er 23:00 nå, lit senere i dagen, og Sjur og jeg har fikk en andre interest vi har i sammen: musikk! Han spieler trumpet og violin, og har en flink øre og lese musikk stykker!).

Sjur Heimdal's farm, Flåm, Norge

THE DRIVEWAY OF THE HEIMDAL FARM

SJUR

When I told him about my singing contests and many solos, he asked me to sing something for him. I chose "Annie's Song" by John Denver, and now he wants to write it down and learn it. He would like me to teach him a new American song every night! Not a problem! Ahh, I think it is very nice to be here with Sjur and his smiling eyes that brighten my day (Å det er moro å bo her med Sjur og han behagelig smil og øyene som lysne opp min dagen!). God Natt!

Saturday, May 20, 1978:

Hallo, hallo! This was a busy day. I slept late, until 9:00, then walked to the grocery store for new ideas in the kitchen. I cooked fishsticks, fried potatoes and eggs (Jeg kokt fiskekaker, poteter og egg). Sjur rubbed his stomach and said it tasted very good (Sjur sa at han spiste godt, og da det smakte deilig). I cleaned the dishes and floors (jeg må vaskes opp nå), and proceeded to make chocolate chip cookies without the chips (shaved a chocolate bar) and strange ingredients (rice-shaped brown sugar?) in the Celsius oven (oops I'm sorry I flunked Celsius 101). They taste ok but they are probably hard enough to break a tooth! Sjur is actually eating them; I can hear the cr-r-r-unch across the house!

When Sjur asked me about my dad, I felt like the words just weren't right when I tried to describe him. I should have held up a mirror to Sjur and said that he was seeing someone pretty close to Dad's kindness, patience, love of animals, pride in family and farming, and good humor. Maybe that's why I feel so comfortable here! He just shook his head sadly when I told him that Dad had his passport ready, and would be at my side in Norway this summer, meeting cousins and touching the ground where his father was a boy. What can you say to that? It was a wonderful dream, never meant to be.

Sjur showed pictures of his parents. His father died in 1960, his mother in 1970. They both lived in this house when it was located further up the Valley. Sjur's guest room is alive with Norsk history & culture! There was a Norwegian version of Steinbeck's "Grapes of Wrath," and plays by Ibsen. There were wooden pictures on the wall with intricate carved landscapes, and paintings by a talented friend from England who visits him each summer. He showed me the 1941 ID of his grandfather when the Germans attacked Norway in WWII. Also, he has the shawl used for baptisms for many children in his family, and the aged white silk "buna" (veil cap) worn by his mother when she married.

We took a drive to the church where Sjur's grandparents, parents, and uncle are buried, then we drove up to the largest waterfall in the Flåm fjellene (mountains). It is the Rørangen Fossen and it is huge and spectacular!

Sjur asked if I saw the "FosseGrimen;" he's the troll who lives in the waterfall and makes music with a magic violin. He has long hair and a big nose, and many famous Norsk composers (Ole Bull, Grieg, Nordraak) have this troll to thank for ideas on writing their new songs!

We talked about Sjur visiting America, which he got pretty excited about, so we opened a map and went over many routes that he could take and visit everyone (including me!). He asked me to describe the farms, weather, roads and cities in the States. I think it's hard for Norwegians to grasp the wide-open spaces, and looong distance between east and west coast. How is it that someone like me has not seen every state? Some folks have the notion that they can be in New Jersey one day, and easily travel to visit California cousins the next day.

(Favorite phrase of the day: "Jeg blir skjelven fra så mye kaffe," (I get the shakes from too much coffee).

Sunday, May 21, 1978 (Søndag 21 Mai):

I have just finished washing the dishes of the best meal I have ever made in any country! We put some meat (Sjur didn't know what kind - kanskje sheep eller deer) in some brun sauce (gravy) and then I grated and sliced fresh carrots and boiled them with potatoes and stirred it all together in the gravy. For dessert, we had ice cream and chocolate (is og sjokolade) syrup, and peaches! Num!

One of the sheep is expecting to give birth to twins any time now! Sjur wants me to stay close to home, because he may need my help if she has trouble. Spennende!!

Sjur has a lot of work planned for us tomorrow, and he told me to get to sleep early. Det er klokka elev nå (it's 11:00 now). He surprised me when he turned the TV on (he usually reads at night) and asked me if I knew who was singing. Of course, it was Petula Clark, singing all the songs I know so well! Her show lasted a half-hour, and I felt like singing along (but I didn't).

Monday, May 22, 1978:

A "Hus-Mor" came by today...Sjur says she goes by the homes in the area and helps any way she can. She gave me a break from the kitchen and made middag for us today; very nice! I worked every muscle I have today. I helped Sjur carry old heavy planks from his old barn, load them on his wagon and then unload them in a new pile. Uffda, det var tung (heavy)! Sjur says I'm sterk (strong).

Next, I hoed the weeds out of his strawberry patch, and then I had 200 cabbages to plant! Well, I got about 70 in the ground in two hours, then Sjur came to help; he does everything so quickly that it didn't take long to plant the rest! I don't know how he goes at the pace he does all day; he's like a machine! I can hardly move my big toe right now without hurting, and he's still jogging circles around me.

Tuesday, May 23, 1978:

Sue, Shelly, and Matt are back in Flåm after touring the Bergen area. They stopped in to say "hi" this morning, and Sue asked if I would mind letting her come and cook a meal for us; she wants to experience a Norsk kitchen! Would I mind!?! Would I mind!?! Heck, this is great! I'm not a natural at this cooking business and it's a relief when someone else does it! I took a lamb roast out of the freezer, and she'll be by to cook it tomorrow.

This afternoon, I helped Sjur move sheep from one pasture to another. These wooly guys have a stubborn mind of their own; they knew I was a stranger so they were scared of me, and they ran all over the place, except through the gate where we were trying to steer them. Finally, I discovered the trick of *The Salt Block*. With a salt block in your hands, you can accomplish anything with sheep. You hypnotize one with the block, and he will follow you anywhere, and his sheep friends will all follow him, because that's what sheep do!

Tonight, we gave birth to twins! Everything went ok, so I just watched the miracle and Sjur let me take a picture of the babies. In all my years back home on the farm, Dad never let me see the baby calves coming into this world. Our mama cats found good hiding places when their time came, so this was really an eye-opener for me! Ouch, it's got to hurt mama sheep when those little hooves come out!

Newborn babies!

Onsdag, 24 Mai:

It was a rainy day in Flåm Valley...nature played a trick and put fog where the mountains used to be. My head hurt most of the day, for no reason. I thought some fresh air would help, so Sjur let me take his bicycle for a ride when the rains slowed down. I rode down to the store to mail my dozens of postcards, including cards to my Vinstra relatives and Alma Skaaden, and Ingebjørg & Halvor in Oslo: Look Out, that crazy American cousin is on her way!

Sue, Shelly, and Matt were late and I knew Sjur didn't want to wait too long, so I took a deep breath and talked myself through my first roasted lamb. I buttered the top, seared it, put spices and water in the bottom of the pan, and threw it in the oven. When Sue came, she put carrots & onions in the pan, and she talked me through my first mashed potatoes, too! So many "firsts" for me in Norway!

Nobody stuck around to help clean up after the meal; it took me two solid hours and my headache was hanging in there. Sjur didn't need me outside, so I snuggled in and worked on my Norway poem that started dancing through my head when I was planting cabbages. I also wrote a little ditty about Sjur:

A velvet voice
and soft-spoken eyes;
an oval smile,
a mind which tries,
hands of a farmer,
patience of a saint;
his life is Portrait Gentle;
his days are strokes of paint.
(Til Sjur Nilsen Heimdal: en dikt av dikter Sherie L. Kleven, May 24, 1978)

Like most folks who wonder why I write endlessly in you, DJ, Sjur's curiosity got to him and he asked about my "skriving." I told him that I just love to write, especially about unique experiences that I never want to forget; it's like an on-going storybook, full of real, colorful characters! I told him I wrote a little poem about him, so he asked to read it. He just smiled, chuckled, and blushed a bit, and he said I am "clever to write"!

Torsdag, 25 Mai:

If anyone ever asks me again if I would help plant cabbages, leeks, or lettuce, I will run for the hills! No, really, it's not so bad; it makes the day go faster than days like yesterday. I can belt-out tunes as loud as I want in that big garden, and no one will be disturbed except the sheep! I put in over six hours, singing, weeding, planting 150 leek, 60 cabbages, and 50 lettuce.

On top of all that, DJ, I pulled-off a good middag: meatloaf, veggies, and french fries! Sjur was amused by the green peas decorating the inside of the meatloaf. Why did I do that? I guess I thought the loaf needed a little something extra, so why not? We had chocolate pudding for dessert. Not bad, ey?

I felt much better today because I slept through a whole night, without waking up to see if time was still awake. This fresh mountain air is making my dreams go crazy; my head takes me back to old times and people that I haven't thought of for years, and mixes them up with new stuff. I wish I could record these dreams!

It's 9:00 p.m. now and Sjur just came in, we are watching the news on TV. There was a bad accident near Laerdal today...a bus met a truck with a trailer on a curve, the trailer broke loose from the truck and smashed into the left side of the bus, killing seven Americans and hospitalizing the rest. Wow, these people were probably having the time of their life, like me, and POOF! Snuffed-out in an øyeblikk.

We had just shut-off the TV, put our yawns on a leash and dragged them into the kitchen. I deflated onto a chair by the table, and Sjur asked, "What did you write in your "Nothing Book" today?" He got some chocolate pudding from the fridge and sat down across from me. He wondered if I wrote poems on my postcards to people (no), and then he asked me what I was humming while I was doing dishes today, and I couldn't remember which of the many songs it could be. He says I have a mezzo-soprano voice.

He also said that I am clever to work, because I got everything done, plus some, which he wanted me to, today. I feel sad about leaving him next week, just when we're really getting synchronized. There's something very captivating about Sjur, and I can't put my finger on one thing. Everything about him is comfortable. His hands are strong and have absorbed years of dirt as proof of their wear. His smile is cute and quick and often focused down or away, in a shy-sort-of style. He has laugh crinkles around his eyes and subtle dimples. He's thin but not lanky, probably 5'10" or 5'11', and very huggable, and his humor is just like mine; we often laugh at the same, precise moment as if it were rehearsed!

Fredag, 26 Mai:

I thought a lot about Dad and Mons today. After washing middag dishes, I grabbed a few moments of meditation and parked myself on the stone wall on the hill overlooking the house, the railroad tracks, and the road. It's $3\frac{1}{4}$ months since Dad died, and it feels like years. It hurts to know that I can't go back home and tell him all about this trip. He would love hearing the details more than anyone I know, and he would want me to tell them over and over again: all about Norwegian farms, what kind of roads, what kind of crops, the equipment, the animals, the food, the weather, the people and exact details on what they did and where they were from . I dream about sitting across from Dad at our table on the farm, and watching him listen.

Sjur reminds me so much of Dad in how he listens and reacts; he often looks away or down, as if focusing his ears on my voice, and smiles gently; now and then chuckles, often shrugs his shoulders when perplexed or in doubt....*so much like DAD!* He loves looking at maps and discussing mileage; loves baked potatoes, chocolate pudding, a clean and organized house; he must be busy all the time, and when there's free time, he reads, or talks with someone - always agreeable and soft-spoken... *so much like DAD!* His face shape, his receding hairline, the crinkles branching from his eyes, his slightly crooked, kind of foxy grin are *so much like DAD!* He peels his potatoes and piles the peelings neatly at the side; he goes after each meal with concentration and gusto, but never rude or sloppy...*just like DAD.* He will sacrifice a good night's sleep to make sure an animal is safe and comfortable...*just like DAD.*

The reason God took Dad and Mons away from me, is just as mysterious as why I ended up on this wonderful farm with an angel in bib over-alls. None of it makes sense to the logical half of my brain, but the spiritual half thinks there's something kind of magical going on here, and I like to imagine my dad's spirit looking over me as I stumble along, trying to figure it all out...

A couple days ago, when Sjur asked about Dad's life and his quick death, I mentioned that the only complaint Dad ever made was that his legs hurt. Sjur said that folks with high blood pressure often feel it in their legs or arms; the aching is from the veins shrinking due to high cholesterol. Interessant. Nobody's explained it to me like that before.

My sad mood disappeared tonight when Sjur said he had a trick to show me with numbers. It was a tic-tac-toe kind of trick (with 5 numbers square) and I figured it out, so then he set up another one and just smiled. I scratched my head and just couldn't get it. Sjur said it takes a good brain and he wasn't going to "learn it" to me. It will remain a mystery! He did say he might write to me with the solution after I'm back home in America.

Sjur really liked dinner tonight ("You're getting more and more clever to cook, I think!"). I made lamb stew; I put everything in it: left-over gravy, carrot slices, potatoes, peas, onions, osv, osv! I was surprised at how delicious it was. Jackpot!

He made a deal with me: he would play his violin if I would let him read more of my poetry. Ok! So, first he played a pretty song about a man walking out of the forest in early morning and seeing the sunrise ("Det Lisnet i Skogen"). Next, a song about spending Sunday with a girl up at the high mountain seter ("Seter Jentens Søndag). Finally, a song about a boy picking a rose ("Heiden Roslein"). The violin makes such soulful, sad notes. It's very beautiful and I could listen forever!

In exchange, I let him read my Norway poem which he studied closely, and asked if I really felt that way about Norway (yes, absolutely!). Then, to lighten the moment, I showed him my mad poem about Brad, and he just smiled and shook his head. He asked if there are any other authors in my family (no, not past or present). That's just one more proof that the stork dropped me at the wrong house! I don't look, act, think, or communicate like any of them...they're all practical, business-like, conservative. Me, I'm creative, impulsive, emotional, goofy!

Saturday, May 27, 1978:

Hei du! Today, I was a painter, a sheep-herder, a gardener, a cook, and a singer. Sjur is building a closet on to my room and he asked me to paint the inside walls and ceiling. Next, I grabbed a salt block and outsmarted the sheep who outsmarted me last time around, and they have a new, fresh patch of grass to thank me for! I watered all the baby grønnsaker, standing tall and proud in an army of green rows. I can't believe we planted all that!

Tonight's dinner was a case of "Øyene vil ha mer enn magen," (the eyes are bigger than the stomach). I made spaghetti and I made sooo-tooo-much! Sjur, when he finally managed to finish his "mighty meal," leaned back and teased, "What shall we have for dessert?' and I just rolled my eyes and said "Uffda!"

After dishes, he took his violin out and asked me to sing "Edelweis" and "Annie's Song" again, so he could learn it on violin. Wow. It's a little intimidating, singing with a beautiful violin. The human voice sounds so weak next to an instrument that reaches down and touches your soul.

There is some kind of enchanting spell which is cast on an experience just before that experience comes to an end, making it very difficult to leave. Whether it's a walk with a friend, a visit home, a 4-month semester, or a trip to Norway, the last moments are immensely magical. Sub-consciously, do people bring out their very best at the tail end so that any negative experiences will be diluted or forgotten?

Three days from now, an east-bound train will take me away from Heimdal gården, to meet new people in Vinstra. I will be very sad to know that I may never see Sjur again. It's incredible (merkelig!) how attached I feel after only two weeks! There were rare moments when the work was exhausting and I plotted my escape (not really), but even then, my heart felt full and alive and happy!

Søndag, 28 Mai:

Time for a sunny Sunday drive! Sjur took us high in the mountains overlooking the "flott utsikt" (fantastic view) of the Flåm valley. Most marvelous was the Berekvam elvegjel: a canyon, *deep*, between the mountains, where the river drops and rushes through, boiling madly all the way!

One of the high mountain farms was home to gobs and gobs of goofy goats - furry, spotted, brown, white, bearded, balding, one-horned - all kind of hanging-out in the middle of the road. They scolded us as Sjur slowly worked his car through the stubborn, funny faces!

He pointed-out a small, abandoned house on the mountain side where a man named Kleiven used to live, and we wondered if he was related to me? Unfortunately, Sjur didn't remember his first name.

Next, we drove by the childhood home of Sjur's mom (Berekvam farm). As we worked our way further down the mountain, Sjur pointed out a cabin where he & his parents hid when the Germans bombed the valley in World War II. Sjur was just a little boy then, but he remembers seeing the planes flying in, lower than the mountains, and sometimes the Germans would search on foot through the mountainside for anyone hiding.

Now, post-war Flåm is quiet, unhurried, far away from the stress of the outside world. The higher you go in the mountains, the more peaceful it is (especially if you love goats). Each farmer,

on average, owns 40 goats. Sjur said the three largest goat farmers work together each summer and take all their goats up to a huge "seter" (summer farm). They usually have at least 250 goats there at one time, and they spend the summer making lots and lots of cheese.

Mondag, 29 Mai:

Det er klokka 24:45 nå og jeg må sove snart (it's past midnight and I must sleep soon)! My time here is running out quickly, and I want to be awake as much as I can. My gut has an unhappy, inside-out kind of pain, anticipating the "good-byes" that are around the corner. Not much I can do about it; I can't freeze time, and I don't think Mom would like it very much if I cancelled my return flight!

I was alone most of today, because Sjur had business errands in Aurland. The sunshine was warmer than most of my days here, so I celebrated by parking myself on a warm rock and reading the latest National Geographic. The pages transported me to another country, far away, and I was traveling across Australia with a woman and her four camels and her dog!

I snapped back to reality in time to make middag for Sjur. Unfortunately, he returned from Aurland much later than planned, and by then, the mashed potatoes were sticky and dry and the breaded torsk had nearly lost its bread...only the grønnsaker were edible!

I baked cookies this afternoon and did it right, not so much of that strange brown sugar that turns cookies into rocks! Sjur will have a couple dozen to munch on, in remembrance of me.

Tonight, we compared childhood in Norway with childhood in America. He thinks kids in the States are forced to grow up too quickly and miss a full, magical childhood. I think high school in Norway is better than America, because they prepare kids for life with a variety of classes, languages, arts, and special on-the-job training. By the time Norwegian kids go to college, they have a clear idea of who they want to be, instead of many American kids, blindly stabbing in the dark at any old major and wasting time with classes that are not steering them toward a compatible career.

This goodbye really hurts

Tirsdag, 30 Mai:

I'm on a lonely east-bound train…it's the wee hours of the morning; my companions are rows of empty seats and there's nothing to see outside the window except memories. There's only one thing worse than goodbyes, and that is saying goodbye when your body clock says it's time to relax and go night-night in the safe, cozy bed that you know, to wake up to the comfortable faces and places that have won your heart. With <u>great</u> reluctance, I must take off my farm-girl hat and put on my traveling hat and carry-on…

My last day på Heimdal gården was a very anxious, sensitive one. I felt like crying much of the time…what made matters worse was the last minute change of plans that forced me to leave about eight hours earlier than planned, because the bus I needed doesn't run until June 5. I was planning to see new scenery, by taking the ferry from Flåm to Kaupanger and a bus from there to Vinstra.

So, the day was full of "last things." It was my last walk through the pasture, last look at the baby sheep, last time watering the garden, last middag (laupskaus, cooked carrots, ice cream). I

This Norskie porch feels like home!

packed my suitcase and tried to wash off the jitters before saying goodbye to my room, and settling downstairs to enjoy one last evening with Sjur. We fixed a traditional Norsk meal of rømmegrøt with flatbrød (Mom would have loved this!). Sjur asked about my future plans, about my family, about my North Dakota farm...we've talked about this before but I guess he just wanted to hear it again...we looked over his family pictures again, and I showed him the pictures in my billfold. With a wink, he said that now I can go back and fix a meal for min kjæreste (sweetheart) that is good for any hard-working man. When I said I don't have a "kjæreste," he asked, "Who is Brad?" and I told him that Brad is a good friend and even a better chef; he wouldn't be happy with the common foods that I know how to fix. Then, I kicked myself many times because that stupid statement was a left-handed insult to Sjur, who likes my plain and simple cooking.

We talked about the route I could take, next time I visit Norway. First, I'd see Telemark again, then Stavanger, then more of Bergen, then Sjur and the Flåm Valley, and finally, Trondheim. I feel sooo at-home in this country; I could live here! I think I should bounce that idea around a little more seriously when it's graduation time!

I didn't know until the last minute that Sjur was paying for my 220 Kroner train ride. That was very unexpected! It really eased the financial stress I was feeling! He said it was nice to have me around, and I must come back! Of course, how could I stay away!?

I gave him a little hug (I would have scared him if I had hugged him as hard as I wanted to!), and climbed onto the train which was right on time at three minutes past midnight. As it chugged along up to Myrdal, I felt like a lost orphan, shivering alone in

THE SNOWY MYRDAL STATION

the night. Sometime after Myrdal, the rocking of the tracks became a lullaby and I managed to sleep for a couple hours.

Wednesday, May 31, 1978:

It is 7:40 a.m. and my mouth is super dry, my left arm, wrist and fingers are on their death-bed from lugging my 100-pound suitcase, and *dropping* the damn thing *loudly* in the middle of the Oslo train station (we Amerikansk tourists really know how to get attention, vet du!). I am making a noble effort to get to Vinstra at the time I promised min slektinger (my relatives). I am, miraculously, on the northbound train to Vinstra. I think it's time for a little shut-eye, if I can...

My warm and funny Bakken cousins

Vel! Hallo, DJ; det er lit senere i kvelden (later, in the evening), and I'm so glad that I'm here! I'm having such a great time; everyone in this Bakken family seems to get a kick out of me... they just watch me and smile, or chuckle at my miniscule Norsk vocabulary...I'm good entertainment, i all fall!

When I first stepped off the train in Vinstra, one of the conductors came up to me and asked if he could help me. How nice! He called my relatives, and in a few minutes, my chariot arrived, driven by Magne Bakken (cute and charming) and his young nephew, Per. They both have red hair and freckles, friendly eyes and quick smiles which immediately strike one's favor. Per is "flink på Engelsk" and we had a fun drive up - up - up the mountain.

We finally reached their farm, where there are two houses and lots of other storage buildings. Here, I met Berthe - they call her Biste (she is my dad's first cousin, because she's the daughter of Grandpa Even's sister Anna). Berthe is 89 years old! She lives in the old house, by herself. Pål Bakken (who drove me up to the Kleven farm two years ago) lives downstairs in the newer house with his wife, Astrid. Pål is Berthe's son. Magne (pronounced Mung-nuh) is the son of Pål and Astrid; he lives upstairs with his wife, Eva, their 2-year old daughter, Ingunn, and they are expecting another child in September.

Magne, Per and Eva are my translators, but when they leave the room, I manage to carry on a fairly decent conversation with the "ekte Norskies"! Pål, Astrid, Berthe and I had been sitting at the big wooden table for quite awhile without a lull when Eva walked back in and Pål told her that we were getting along fine because I am so "flink på Norsk!". I wish Sjur could hear me now; he would be proud!

Magne is a real estate agent, Eva is a first-grade teacher (she has a class of 15 students). Berthe is your typical fairy-tale grandmother - sweet, giggly, cozy, generous; Astrid is boisterous, assertive but good-natured, and Pål is a soft-spoken, hard working farmer.

We compared prices and wages; a small Ford in Norway costs 75,000 kroner. That's $15,000! Yikes! You can buy one in the States for a third of that price. Also, Eva and others think nothing of being paid the equivalent of $10 an hour or more (U.S. minimum wage is $2.90 now!). They also save money because they don't have to pay medical costs; the government covers that for everybody.

Everything here is home-grown or self-made, from the food on the table to the happy little still, brewing "heim-brennt" fire water (one whiff will cure anything), to the "heim-rolled sigaretter" (smokes with no filter). I think my throat and my lungs have first-degree burns from sampling both those goodies!

Magne and Eva will soon outgrow their cozy quarters upstairs. It's really cute how Eva has decorated it, especially the red and white kitchen, complete with a red refrigerator and checkered curtains. They took me for a drive around the mountains, which are more gentle and sloping than the rugged, rocky Flåm mountains. They played some tapes of American singers; Magne likes American country music and also Elvis Presley. We saw a moose and I was so excited because I've never seen a moose in person! They laughed when I told them that big men with big guns go moose-hunting back home...you see, DJ, "moose" på Norsk means "mouse"! Let's go mouse-hunting!

We drove about 10 Km north to Kvam, to the home of Magne's sister Bjørg, her husband Åd and their son, Per. We had snacks and coffee on their porch in the cooling but never cold Norsk night air. I am treated so well by this wonderful family. Magne is such a tease; he says the reason I like Norway so much is because of that bachelor farmer (ugift bonden) in Flåm, and there will be a wedding (bryllup) next summer! Bare tulle prat (silly talk)! Then, my night without sleep started punishing me with a headache (høde-pene). Åd gave me some kind of seltzer tablets, and the pounding drum went away (I should take some of these back home with me).

Torsdag, 1 Juni:

Jeg sov som en stein i hele natt siste kveld (I slept like a stone the whole last night) and woke up at 11:30! Flott! Eve, Ingunn and I had a breakfast of puffed rice, marmalade, and lefse.

Berthe asked me to come outside with her, and we sat together on the wooden bench by her house, watching Ingunn play in the grass. We talked as much as we could, and when words wouldn't do, it was wonderful to simply sit there and soak up the sun.

Berthe Bakken & Ingunn

Eva came out with a box of old photographs. Berthe was feeling too warm, so she took a chair and set it in the shade inside her door, and Eva and I settled just outside the door on her front step. As Berthe picked each picture out of the box, Eva translated who they were. Suddenly, before my very eyes there was a good, studio picture of Even Kleiven, min bestefar (grandpa)! Spennende!! How I wish Dad could be here now to see this picture of his young father, along with his aunts and uncles! Berthe saw the tears in my eyes, and told me to keep this picture; wow, I didn't know what to say. The only other existing picture of Even is a warped, faded, rained-on mess in our attic. This is too cool! What a trip, what a trip. My heart is feeling the old Norge and the new Norge and I don't know which I love more!

Tonight, Astrid had a "kvinne-klub" meeting at her house. This was like a Ladies-Aid meeting only without the Bibles. About 15 or 20 women ate snacks, sang songs, and played a game where they picked numbers and paid 50 øre for each and somehow won little prizes. Berthe was so sweet; she gave me 2 Kroner to try and win, but no luck. The ladies snacked and talked, talked, talked...so much to say, so fast, so loud! Magne and Per came to save me from the scene to go "moose hunting," but no luck there, either. Where are all the moose!?

One thing that's the same here as in Amerika is that I do enjoy the company of men more than the women! Thanks to hanging out with my dad, I'm just one of the guys (with a little flirtation added in)!

When we got back to the house, it was almost 11:00 and the women's group was finally breaking up. Eva, Magne and I moved upstairs to wind-down. We shared a little home-brew and sang party songs to each other. I wrote down the verses to one of

my favorites, about a man who has no farm, no money, no woman, no property, but he is happy because he finds gifts in the earth, sun, flowers, stars. It's called "Og Jeg har ingen Bondegård," and I hope I can remember the melody!

It's 1:30 a.m. now and I must close my eyes on my last evening at this wonderful place.

Fredag, 2 Juni:

Here I sit at the train station at 8:25 a.m., crying. Goodbyes, yuck. We woke up at 6:30, and after a shower and a light frøkost, I felt like Dorothy saying goodbye to her Oz friends. Pål, Astrid, Berthe and Eva all lined-up by the door to shake hands and give me one last smile. Magne og Per kjørte meg ned til stasjonen...and here I am. The last thing Magne said is that they hope to see me again in one year. I hope so, too!

Later....it is 4:00 in the afternoon and I'm in the Lillehammer bus station, waiting to ride up to Alma's. I have spent the last three hours on a little Lillehammer shopping spree, and I feel much better now! I found perfect little tokens for everyone: a Krims-Krams jar for Brad, a traditional silver brooch for Mom, a happy little dancing troll pin for Mari, and a couple thank-you cards for Sjur and my Vinstra slektinger. I splurged almost $20 on myself with a cute, clunky pair of brown/tan clogs, on sale for *bare nytti kroner!* I just finished a soft ice cream cone, and I feel very satisfied and looking forward to seeing Alma again.

Hi DJ, it's 10:30 and I am tucked under the soft blankets on Alma's couch; the moon is peeking through the bottom tassel on her window shades, and I hear the Norwegian crickets singing outside.

SHOPPING FOR SHOES?

It's probably good that my visit here is short, because Alma isn't as healthy as she was two years ago. She is now 76 years old; she rubs her legs a lot and says, "jeg har vondt i benet og kan ikke gå for longt," which means the pain in her legs stops her from moving around like she used to. She doesn't smile quite as much or giggle like she used to (because of pain?) but she is still very koselig (cozy) and patient. Thanks to my growing vocabulary, it was a little easier for us to talk this time. When I told her that she could have been meeting my dad this summer, but God had other plans, she shook her head sadly. She opened her Bible and talked about the promise of heaven. She also talked about Moses and how his faith was tested. I think Alma has very strong faith. She showed me her church newsletter with pictures of the choir, pastor, and a new center they built for young girls in trouble.

While she fixed a snack for us, she pointed to her stack of 45's records and said I could play anything I wanted. They were all religious songs, but it was fun playing with the old phonograph. When we sat down to eat, I told her that I could say part of the Norwegian table prayer, but I didn't know the whole thing. Wow, what a smile, what light in her eyes! She took my hands in hers, and we said the prayer together. Can any words describe that moment? Our two souls jumped across the ocean, across generations, meeting over sandwiches and cookies in a humble little kitchen that suddenly seemed to hold all the answers to eternity.

"I Jesu navn går vi til bord
og spise, drikke på dit ord,
deg Gud til ære, oss til gavn,
så får vi mat I Jesu navn.
For mat og drikke her du gav,
for din velsignelse der av,
for daglig brød fra Faderhånd,
lær oss å takke ved din ånd."

Gloria and Sherie

My heart was overflowing, but my stomach was starving! We dried our eyes and filled our plates. As we ate, she talked about her sisters, Bina and Hanna, who live here in the city and are in their 80's. They see each other every week. She asked if I was close to my sisters and I told her the truth, that Gloria and I connect pretty well despite the 13-year age difference, but it seems that LaVonne would have been much happier if I had never been born. Alma said she hopes that will change as we get older.

We walked around her flowering yard and settled-in the metal lawn chairs by her rose bushes and watched the setting sun. She remembered our first meeting, two years ago when I backpacked all 4 miles uphill to her house. She thought it was "skrekkelig og forferdelig (horrible and dreadful)! I definitely had more spunk that summer!

Five hours with her flew by, and it was time to say goodnight. I will be leaving for Oslo, bright and early in the morning. I wish I had thought to bring a little gift to her; she is so sweet and she deserves a pick-me-up. How stupid of me not to think of that.

Saturday, June 3, 1978:

It's 9:35 a.m. now and I'm waiting for my train to Oslo. I left Alma's at 6:30 this morning and I walked...and walked...and walked down to the tog stasjon (train station). I think this doggone suitcase is heavier than the backpack I had two years ago. The handle should have snapped off by now and my knuckles should be scraping the ground from the weight of it stretching my arm out! I could have taken the bus this morning, but I really wanted to walk and breathe in everything about an early Lillehammer morning. The first couple miles were somewhat magical, and then it just became work!

413

Johnnie from Hallingdal

Wow DJ, dette turen er bedre og bedre dag for dag (this trip gets better every day)! I had planned to simply arrive in Oslo, meander around a bit and then connect with Ingebjørg and Halvor. Nope, the troll of the railway had other plans for me! When the train stopped in Hamar this morning, a young guy came on and sat by me. He introduced himself as Johnnie from Hallingdal (southeast of Bergen), he spoke English very well, and we chatted about lots of odd-ball things for the next couple hours. When we disembarked at the Øst Stasjon in Oslo, he asked what I would do, and I shrugged my shoulders. He only came for the fun of it, a change of scenery, with no agenda other than to have a nice meal, and he asked if I would have dinner with him. He helped me cram my monstrous suitcase in a locker and we stepped out into the Oslo air, heading for no place in particular.

Of all the guys I've met on this trip, Sjur is probably the most honorable and least intimidating. I got exactly the same vibe from Johnnie. It seemed perfectly natural to just "be" with him. His stature and mannerisms remind me a lot of my farmer friend from Cooperstown, Keven Lunde. Johnnie is small in stature, with blonde, loose curls, glasses and an easy smile. He's intelligent, well-read, good-humored and very relaxing to talk with; kind of like a brother.

The last time he was in Oslo was January, and he apologized for not knowing his way around very well but I reassured him that I'm not afraid of getting lost, in fact I find it an adventure! We lucked-out after walking only a few blocks, and found a very nice restaurant, three stories up in an office building. The meal

JOHNNIE!

was very good: carbonade og grønnsaker (hamburger steak and vegetables) with vannbakkels (cream puffs) for desert.

We swapped stories and I learned that he is 19 years old, which surprised me because he seems older; he has his act together better than most 19-year-olds I know! He is a student and a worker. He has three more years of school to become a "high-class" mechanic (his words). He works in a factory and has a nice apartment in Hallingdal; his rent is only 300 Kroner per month (ikke so dyrt)! In his spare time, he likes to read. I told him that I like to write in my spare time. He wanted to read something by me, so I shared my Norge poem with him and he said when I make a book, I must send it to him!

We each lost our internal compass when we walked out of the restaurant...hey, the Øst Stasjon moved while we weren't looking! It was fun and we laughed a lot and finally got ourselves un-lost. I took a picture of Johnnie in front of the Øst Station, and it was time to say our "Ha Dets" before he boarded his train for home. I said, "Jeg var heldig å møte deg i dag," and he said, "Ikke so..." and kissed my cheek, and he was gone, leaving me with that old familiar lump in my throat.

Saturday night in Oslo

I started walking in the general direction of the Hotel Scandinavia, but when I never saw it looming above any nearby buildings, I "unnskylded" (excuse-me?) a man walking by with his young son. As it turned out, the man was from England, has lived in Norge for two years, as a technician. As a light rain began to fall, he was very nice to walk with me, his son on a little tricycle beside us, until he could point, precisely, to my destination. I thanked him (mange, mange tusen takk!) and we parted ways. Again, I marvel at how lucky I have been on this trip to meet so many special people!

Ingebjørg and Halvor didn't answer their phone (I told them in my postcard that I would call them either today or tomorrow), so I paced for a while, tried again, with no luck. It was raining and I just wanted to relax and warm up. Thanks to Sjur, I had enough money for a cheap room, so I walked to the Forbunds Hotel and rented room #314 for about $45. It wasn't very fancy; the view was the alleyway and the walls were bare.

I felt much better after a hot shower and new clothes. In fact, I felt brave. It was Saturday night in Oslo! I pulled out the phone number for that Rolando guy from my first night here. What the heck, I thought, let's have another little eventyr (adventure) in people. I had no phone in my room, so I walked down to the pay phone. It was 5:30 in the afternoon, and he was home. Yes, he remembered me, yes he would like to meet me "og gå på kino og Singapore Slings og så videre (and so on)." It was the "og så videre" that made my heart tilt sideways a little. This guy definitely wasn't the safe, brotherly Johnnie-type. He said he would come to my hotel room, but I said I wanted to meet him in the lobby of the Hotel Scandinavia.

When I hung-up the phone, I felt kind of numb and stiff, like zombies had taken over my body, and it wasn't the chilly rain. I couldn't breathe! I have a lot of practice in getting together with guys as friends but I've never arranged a date before. Who am I?!? Suddenly, the numb zombie-ness was replaced by pure, jangling, electric nerves. If I could tap into *Star Trek* power, I would have transported myself anywhere comfortable and familiar, like Sjur's kitchen or Alma's back yard!

About an hour later, I had talked myself down from being terrified to being a "flink jente" (clever girl) who would keep her wits about her with this gutt fra Sør Amerika (lad from South America)! Sitting in the lobby at Hotel Scandinavia, writing in you, DJ, suddenly I realized someone was standing in front of me. There he was, with a smile, extending his hand to help me up.

He asked if I would like to see a movie, so we caught "Taxi Driver" with Robert DeNiro. It was weird, because they showed it in the English-speaking version, with Norsk sub-text. It wasn't really my kind of movie; the big climax at the end was a bit too bloody for me, but I guess it was a good story.

As we walked away from the kino, he took my hand, like we were boyfriend-girlfriend, and we made our way back to square one: the Hotel Scandinavia bar/lounge. I only had one drink, and our conversation was comfortable. He held my hand and gradually sat closer to me, putting his arm around my shoulders and brushing my hair, but he was a gentleman. He asked about my experiences on this trip, about my family, and why my grandparents moved to America. I told him about my dad, and he said his father died three years ago, and he missed him. He talked about his home in Columbia, how it's not as liberated as Norway, and women have old-fashioned roles. I found out that his job involves studying various plant, vegetable, crop species (a horticulturalist?). He thinks I've chosen a good career, in Sociology and counseling, because I am so open, honest, and creative. He asked me to describe North Dakota. He has cousins in Canada, California, Florida, New York, and may visit the States next year.

He asked about my writing, and I let him read my Norge poem. He seemed to study it very carefully, and asked me if I really believed what I wrote about being one with the land. Of course

I do! We talked about spirits and spirituality and religion. He asked if I'm very religious and I told him that I really believe in God now, because I feel that He has been with me on this trip, introducing me to special people and places and helping me heal from the death of my dad and my uncle. I added that I am definitely not a puritan, and in my group of church friends, I'm considered one of the wildest ones, but I try not to be stupid about being wild, never doing anything to hurt myself or anyone else. Rolando looked like he was trying to understand, but couldn't quite grasp it.

Finally, it was close to the witching hour, and I said I had to meet my relatives early in the morning (a little fib), so I needed to thank him and call it a night. He leaned in and kissed me and the butterflies in my stomach went flip-flop. He's a verrrry good kisser. Whew! He insisted on walking me back to my room at the Forbunds Hotel, and as we got closer to my room, I got the jitters all over again. I unlocked the door and turned to say thanks but didn't get the words out before he was kissing me again. Yikes! My knees turned to rubber. We paused, there was silence, and he asked if I would forget him for some American guy. Inside my head, I was thinking, yeah, I'm going back to someone who frustrates me (Brad) instead of someone who excites me (you), but I only shrugged my shoulders and said that nothing could erase my memories of the special people on this trip. He backed up just a few inches, and said that perhaps he should try to catch the 12:20 train for home, to write a report that is due on Monday. He looked into my eyes, hoping I would talk him out of it and invite him in (?), he kissed my hand and I thanked him again, wished him luck and slowly backed away into my room.

So. Det var det!

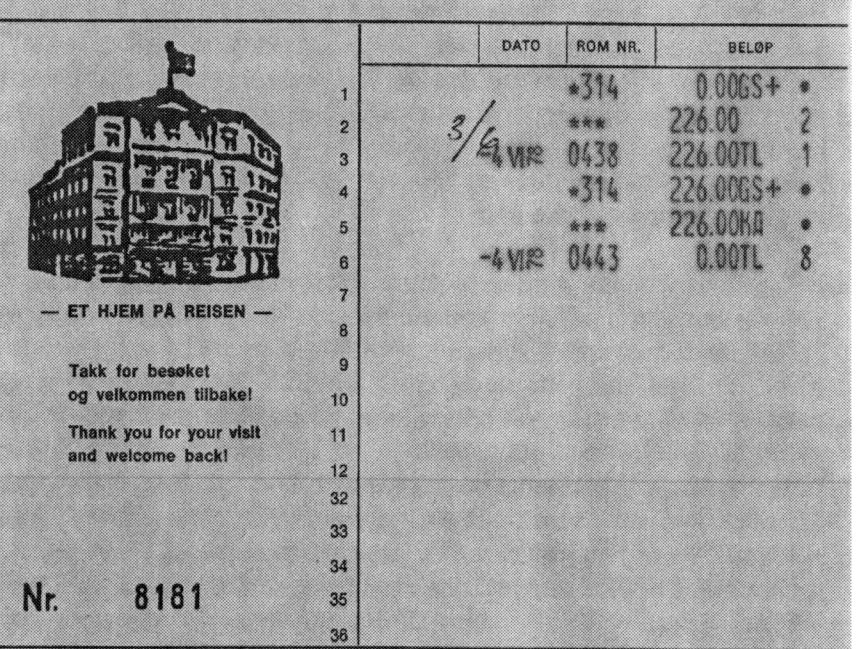

DATO	ROM NR.	BELØP	
	∗314	0.00GS+	∗
	∗∗∗	226.00	2
3/4 VIR	0438	226.00TL	1
	∗314	226.00GS+	∗
	∗∗∗	226.00KA	∗
-4 VIR	0443	0.00TL	8

1
2
3
4
5
6
7
8
9
10
11
12
32
33
34
35
36

— ET HJEM PÅ REISEN —

Takk for besøket
og velkommen tilbake!

Thank you for your visit
and welcome back!

Nr.   8181

Forbundshotellet
Holbergs pl. 1 - OSLO 1 - Tlf. 20 88 55
Bankgiro 9021.07.40383 - Postgiro 210358
Tlgr.adr.: Forbundshotel - Telex 19413

FROKOST INKLUDERT   Breakfast included

Kun maskinstemplede regninger gjelder
som kvittering.

Only bills machineprinted are valid
as receipt.

25 000. 11-77.   O. nr. 4681.

Sunday, June 4, 1978:

It's 8:20 a.m., and I see warm sunshine instead of rain outside my hotel window. I would like to sleep longer, because I am tired from all the adventures yesterday, but my mind is wide awake. I have relived the moments with Rolando, and even though he is a nice person and cute, I just don't feel the strong personality attraction to him as I have with Sjur, Magne, Johnnie...and as there is with Brad and Keven back in the States. I don't feel my heart yearning and praying that I'll hear from him again, as I do with the others. It sure was a fun little fling, though, and I'm glad I didn't do anything to embarrass myself! Oh...P.S., DJ: he left a little souvenir to remember him by. Yup, this late-bloomer just got her first hickey!

Cousin Ingebjørg and Halvor

Hi DJ, it's 11:00 p.m. and I have been at Ingebjørg and Halvor's since noon. It's very nice to see them again; they are the ideal people to be with on my last days in Norge. We comfortably switch from Engelsk to Norsk in all our conversations, and we seem to bring out the laughter in each other.

Ingebjørg showed me how far she is on her family tree project, and she will send copies to me. They had tons of pictures from their trip to the States last summer by Greyhound bus. They actually saw both coasts and the midwest...by bus!?!? That doesn't sound very comfortable to me, but they were thrilled about it! They weren't crazy about New York, but they liked Chicago and San Francisco. They thought Texas was too hot and humid and they were amazed at the big skies and flat ground of the midwest. Ingebjørg said she looked for my name in the phone book in Fargo...shoot, I wish they had told me they were coming! Det var ble spennende å hilse velkommen til meg spesiell slektninger (it would have been fun to welcome my special relatives)!

We had a delicious, light meal of fiskesuppe og flatbrød med hvit vin (fish soup, rye crackers and white wine). Det smakt så godt (yum)! We ate on the balcony of their 12th floor apartment, facing hints of sky beyond the city buildings. As usual, Halvor dominated the conversation, and I enjoy hearing him; he is a very interesting story-teller! He's like the Garrison Keillor of Norway!

They will be going to their cozy farm in Bø later this week, to stay for the rest of the summer. If I had to choose between the two homes, Bø would win, hands-down, because it's such a cozy little farm. This Oslo apartment may be convenient for Halvor's classes at the University, but it does not reflect their cheerful personality like their home in Bø.

Monday, June 5, 1978:

Yikes, DJ, this trip is ending too soon...I want to stay longer, longer, longer! This Norway home has felt so *right*, and now I don't know whether to say I am Amerikansk eller Norsk! When I get back home, I feel like I will look at everything and everybody differently.

My last day was a very nice one. This morning, Ingebjørg and I had a great, fun talk over frøkost...then, we took the underground train to an art museum uptown. I love looking at paintings; it was fascinating. We easily spent three hours there. After the museum, we bought some ice cream and wandered, window-shopping like two girlfriends. We looked at wallpaper samples in a small home-furnishing store, because she is going to change her bathroom. She said I will have to come back next year and see the pattern that I picked, covering their walls!

HAPPY FIDDLER ~OSLO

We grabbed a taxi, and I got lost. I'm not sure which end of town we ended up in, but Halvor was there waiting for us at a smorgasbord. There were fiddlers playing festive songs outside the door, and we made our way in to an incredible display of food! There was steak, potatoes, fish, vegetables, fruits, soups, breads, and all kinds of beverages. Once I discovered the beautiful little crab cakes, I was blind to anything else. They were a yummy little blend of crab, spinach, rice and a cream sauce, tucked in a cake-like box. Wow. Speechless!

"Takk for matt, det var godt; vi er alle mette nå. Bravo, bravo, bravisimo!!"

I _will_ come back!

Tuesday, June 6, 1978:

Ingebjørg woke me at 4:00 a.m., so we could catch the underground train at 5:00 which would take us to the bus stop at Braathen's Safe at 5:45. She and I talked all the way; I get along so well with her! She carried my heavy suitcase a good part of the way, switching with me now and then. She stayed with me at the bus stop as more and more people showed up for the ride to Gardermoen.

Finally, at 6:30, it was time to say goodbye. I didn't feel as emotionally torn-up about leaving, because I _will_ see Ingebjørg again! It is not difficult or expensive to come here (as long as I know Arne Brekke!). I _will_ be back! If I could have stayed longer, I absolutely would have. I would have found a job somewhere and lived happily ever-after! But, alas, the homeland calls...

Our 9:00 a.m. flight out of Gardermoen was delayed until 10:30, so I found a good day-dream corner by a window and just let myself breathe in all the memories.

The troll of the restrooms granted me one last gift before leaving dette spennende landet (this exciting country). I happened to pick a stall which was decorated with graffiti. Another poet had preceded me here, a hopeless romantic, nuts about boys. Here's what this anonymous dikter wrote on the walls:

> "Gutter er som luft -
> Jeg trenger luft for å leve.
> Gutt er som brød -
> og nå er jeg sulten.
> Penger er ikke alt her i livet;
> vi har jo også gutter!"

Translation: Boys are like the air, and I need air to live. Boys are like bread, and now I am hungry. Money is not everything in this life; we also have boys!

> "Takk skal du ha
> og gift skal du bli
> of får du ikke noen annen,
> so skal du få meg!"

Translation: Good luck shall you have, and married shall you be, and if you can find no other, so shall you have me.

Shelly (from the Oslo-Flåm drive with Arne Brekke, so many days ago) sat with me and the 8-hour flight went quickly. We read comic books and glamour magazines, took advantage of the free drinks and hadde det moro (had a good time)! We talked about many things and I really enjoyed her company. She

gave me a bad time because every story I told, had me with a different guy: Brad, Ron, Keven, Paul, Rolando, Johnnie, etc! I told her that I don't try to be a girlfriend to guys, I am just a friend, and so they find me comfortable to be around because it's not complicated...with the exception of Brad, of course...I'm not sure <u>what</u> we are! Shelly is dating a guy named Brad, too. Look out, Shelly!

We landed in Winnipeg at 6:30 p.m. Norsk time, or just after noon Canadian time. It was cold, icey and windy and gave me one more reason to wish I had stayed in Norge. We piled into a bus and headed for Grand Forks. Once the five Norwegians on our bus were cleared at Canadian-US Customs, we were on our way, reaching Grand Forks at midnight Norsk time, 6:00 p.m. US.

That lonely old orphan feeling

I didn't have my key to get in at Flaagan's, and no one was home, but luckily the back door was open. I dragged my suitcase down the stairs and found a stack of mail waiting for me, mostly from all my friends who have moved on to begin new lives and don't even know that I went to Norway. So, what, where, when is *my* new life? That lonely old orphan feeling was looming in the pit of my stomach.

I didn't feel the answers when I opened my confirmation of summer classes at UND, and I didn't feel the answers in the envelope of papers from my new part-time job at S&S Personnel. There definitely weren't answers in the big envelope from Mom; she had forwarded my mail from the farm. At the top of the stack was Mom's letter; I opened it first. It had very few words of her own and many quotes from the sisterhood (Gloria says this...LaVonne says that...). It seems they have dissected my parts and have found a very selfish person, insensitive to others and unreliable. Whoa. I guess I was hallucinating those infinitesimal warm fuzzies when I left on this trip. Ok...scratch the plans for a happy home reunion...deep breath...we've been through this "damage control" before...this is easy to fix. Mom just needs me to "be" with her, to simply hang-out and share the air, and all the pieces fall back into place, leaving no room for cruel and careless chatter (Hellooo, Mom, remember me?? – I've been home more weekends than not – remember me?? – we've stayed up through many strange nights, just Mom and Sherie, quietly contemplating our world without Dad – remember, Mom???). She knows my heart, even now in her deflated, depressed state of mind, she knows me. My sisters...*what* am I going to do with my sisters...I must make a note to never leave them alone without strict adult supervision ever again.

A warm shower may have cleaned me up, but it didn't cheer me up. This just didn't seem right, to come home to apocalyptic silence after a spectacular trip that tickled my soul. Where is the vibrance, the life, the pulse? The sunshine is flat, the colors are sad and sounds are hollow. I walked to Wittenberg Chapel, and the purple walls were still, as if waiting for the familiar voices to return. I needed to see a smile, a friend who understands falling in love with Norway but who will help ease me back into being an American. I called Mari, and she told me to come on over!

My faithful steed, Buford, parked in the chapel lot, looked like a foreign object to me. I just stared at this old brown and chrome friend until my mind clicked on and I climbed inside. He made a dry, scraping sound when I tried to start him up, so I moved my foggy brain in to the chapel and floated out again with a pitcher of water...checked the oil and a half-flat tire and drove him out to Mari's, hoping the tire would hang in there for a few blocks.

Talking with Mari was good for me and good for her. She hasn't been feeling well and she enjoyed being distracted with stories of my trip. She had good advice regarding the sisterhood: because they are married and I am single, they believe that I can more easily drop my commitments and responsibilities. Instead of always telling them how busy I am, she suggested that I curb my words, because they are making a mental check list and comparing what I do back on the farm, compared to what I do in my college life. In their minds, I will always come up short of what they think I should be doing. If they have no details, they have no fuel for their fire; and besides, I don't think they are very interested in my activities, anyway. Let 'em be mushrooms! Keep 'em in the dark!

It was Wednesday, 5:00 a.m. Norsk time, 11:00 p.m. US, when I left Mari's and headed home to Flaagan's; Jim and Jeanette were happy to see me and wanted to hear all about my adventures. My eyes went cross-eyed; I had been awake for 26 hours straight and my old bed looked real good.

Wake up, sleepy American

I slept all morning, and only awoke because my red phone was ringing. It was Bev, from the chapel, wanting to take me out for coffee and lunch. I dropped off my trip pictures at Colormatic, and met Bev at LaCampanã. Yum, my Chimichanga was sooo big and sooo tasty; what a treat! As we talked, I slowly felt the sleeping American waking inside me. Bev thinks that good things happened to me in Norway, for the same reason good things happen to me in the States, and I asked, "Why is that?" She said these special moments happen because I make them happen; my positive approach to life is a magnet for little miracles. She says that I fascinate people and draw them near; I am "vivacious" and people like to stick around and see what exciting things will happen next. She added that sometimes, I

may be too agreeable for my own good, because there are times to say "no" and stick to it, and I need to learn that so folks don't take advantage. Wow. I don't know about all that; I'll have to chew on it for awhile. Has anyone ever taken such a deep look at me before? I think not! She also said that Brad really missed me...he seemed lost without his running-partner (me) and didn't ask to do anything with anybody else; he only stopped for short conversations and kept to himself.

After lunch, I picked up my fantastic, beautiful, perfect photos! I drove by the chapel and saw Pastor Dave's car, so I ran in to say hi! He gave me a big hug, looked at my pics and shared my excitement, hearing me bubble-over with thousands of words! He asked when would I be going home to my mom (tomorrow), and had I seen Brad yet? He sent me on my way, saying that someone out there was going to be very happy to see me...

With the Krims-Krams jar tucked behind my back, I walked across the street and up the stairs. I set the jar on the floor outside his door, knocked, and hid around the corner. He opened it, looked around, picked up the jar, tip-toed to the corner, smiled and ran back inside, shut the door, but two seconds later, opened the door and walked toward me with his arms wide open and gave me the biggest, best hug! His smile said it all; he loved the Krims-Krams jar and immediately stuffed potato chips in it! He was like a little kid at show 'n tell time, leading me from one room to another, see, see - a new suit, a new caftan, his baby photo book which his mom just gave him (there was little Brad, in the early days with the big Spock ears)! We both went on and on and on, and when he asked if Buford was ok, he wanted to go to the Gaslight lounge for a drink. The Oriental Comet Sisters were singing, and it was funny hearing their "clazee" accent on American songs. After one drink, we went back to his place and he made popcorn and we moved into the bedroom, to look at his books. We spent three hours, sitting on his bed, talking about

POOR BUFORD

so many things, I can't remember them all...his family, my family, traveling, friends, carnivals and scary rides ....we laughed a lot, and finally, his voice was hoarse, and it was 4:30 in the morning. I am sure I was glowing so much on my drive home, Buford didn't need his headlights!

Thursday, June 8, 1978:

I fixed Buford's tire this morning, and hit the road for the farm. I stopped at Beaver Creek cemetery to say hi to Dad. Some folks might think I'm crazy for having conversations with him, but it always makes me feel better, so why not?

In the two miles between Beaver Creek and the farm, my stomach mutated into a tight knot of barbed wire, and I bet even Buford wanted to slam it into reverse and head the opposite way. I pulled in, took a deep breath, psyched myself up and bounced through the door. Dan, LaVonne and Mom were sitting around the table, eating lunch and watching TV. Mom said, "You're late," and I started to tell her about the flat tire when Dan piped in, saying if I hadn't been too lazy to get out of bed, I could have gotten the tire fixed early, and been here first thing this morning. LaVonne just kept eating and staring at the TV. Cheez, I didn't have an appointment with them for a specific time; give me a break! I started going into defensive-mode, explaining about jet lag and all, and then I stopped myself, sat down and followed their hypnotic stares into the TV GOD. There were helicopters flying across the screen, but my mind was flying backwards, across the ocean, to Sjur and Alma...and I wondered what they would think of this family in action. I can almost see Sjur, shaking his head in disbelief.

They finished eating and talked amongst themselves about their house-building problems. They went on a bit, then got up and left, asking nothing....*NOTHING* about Norway! Finally, alone

GRANDPA EVEN'S GRAVE, GRYGLA, MN

with Mom, I asked, "Aren't you even glad to see me?" She said, "Sure, but we're so used to you coming and going..." to which I said, "But Mom, this time, I am coming back from *Norway*....I met relatives, I worked on a farm...I was hoping my family would be a little interested!" Mom sighed, started washing lunch dishes, and I just stared at her, waiting....finally, she said we should drive in to Mayville and see Uncle Melvin so that he could hear about his Norway relatives.

Melvin was so wound-up, talking a mile a minute and he hardly could sit still to look at pictures or hear my story. It's always hard to believe that he and my dad were brothers. Melvin is so impatient and opinionated, but he is the only surviving Kleven uncle, so we must make the best of it.

When Mom and I got home, she made my favorite macaroni salad, and then she sat outside in the lawn chair and watched me plant circles of petunias and snapdragons for her. Memories of Sjur's garden were dancing in my head! Next, after I washed-up, Mom washed her hair and I set it in curlers for her. We settled outside again, watching the ground squirrels and talking a little. Mom agrees that these 5 months since Dad died have been like a blur.

This farm is the evidence of my Dad. This is what he did, this is what he created. No one will ever touch this farm or do his chores in quite the same manner ever again. I see the old cobweb-coated contents of the barn, the sagging skeleton of the old, old house which great-grandma Anne from Norge built in 1886. I marvel at the fact that an object with no capacity to love, care, or feel a damn thing, can outlive, so stubbornly, a human with so much to contribute to life.

And so this weekend slipped on into the usual routine with my un-spunky Mom... trips to town for groceries... long walks in the

Macaroni Salad

1 pkg. (7 ounce) Macaroni, 6 eggs hard boiled, Some diced Celery & onion. Can tuna. 1 Can peas (drained).

Boil mac. until tender, drain & add rest of ingredients. Add as much Salad dressing as Needed.

Sliced stuffed Olives are good in it, or relish or sweet pickles.

AUNT CLARA ♡ (with Sherie, below)

cowless pasture... lawn mowing... weeding... TV... sister-family popped in and out to inhale food, exhale their busy-ness (I'm still an invisible ghost).

A bright flicker of hope, wearing baby blue and red hair, pulled in to our yard on Sunday. It was Aunt Clara. She's hurting, too, from losing Mons, but somehow she seems to be able to pull out of it and smile once in a while. She is the only one who can temporarily erase the tired sadness on Mom's face and exercise her smile muscles. She is good for all of us; she is the smallest of us but she has a BIG, towering aura of dignity, kindness and humor. Her open mind reaches out and pulls us into a big family hug. We don't *compete* when Aunt Clara is around; we *share*. That's rare. Aunt Clara isn't related to Alma Skaaden, but I see the same spunk, the giggle, the comforting spirit that teaches us how to simply breathe...and relax...

Maybe that's what it's all about: finding the Alma, the Sjur, the Aunt Clara in ourselves and using it to bring out the best in those around us.

Haystack memories: Sherie, cousins Curt & Burkley Stordahl & Teeny (1966)

Easy day at the river with Ruby, Kevin & baby Simba - 1994

ABOUT THE AUTHOR:

Sherie grew up on the corner of Golden Lake and Beaver Creek Townships, rural Sharon, North Dakota. She earned a B.A. in English and Sociology at UND in 1978, moved to Sacramento, California and spent many years as a work skills counselor/trainer for handicapped adults.

Sherie's first writing for the public eye was through editorials in her high school newspaper. At UND, she won the Gladys Boen Literary Award for poetry in 1976. She continued to write frivolous verse for friends and family until her first poem was published in *Bloodroot* magazine, spring 1978.

Bounced around in the lonely backseat of life, Sherie's muse patiently rode the rough patch of divorce and career changes. After years as a bus driver for the handicapped, Sherie got an office job and now works as a bookkeeper for a tool manufacturer.

Sherie and her cat, ToFisk, married Kevin and his dog, Ashley, in 1987 on the boat *Touché* in the San Francisco Bay. In 1991, they settled in northern Idaho where Ashley and ToFisk's spirits moved on. The family grew with the adoption of three beautiful dogs (Ruby, Simba and Roscoe) and three spunky cats (Sabrina, MeeOdo and Maybelline). They live on a six-acre patch at the western edge of the St. Joe and Coeur d'Alene mountain ranges, where Sherie rediscovered her muse, nestled-in with the native creatures of the pure and mystical woods.

In 2000 and 2001, Sherie published two poems in a compilation by The International Library of Poetry. In 2004, she won first prize in a contest by Innervision Poetry Group in Spokane, WA, which opened the door to this publication, "Beaver Creek Blues."

Sherie can be reached at beavercreek.blues@yahoo.com.

Printed in the United States
67938LVS00003B/32

9 781425 915841